2 Sides 2

the Story

2 Sides 2

the Story

Everyone has their own opinion but let's
not forget the truth

A.M. Locker
C.C. Downer

Published by: Triple Infinity Creations

Triple Infinity Creations, C/o 46 Hawkinge, Gloucester Road, London N17 6LP England, United Kingdom

Triple Infinity Creations Ltd, Registered Offices, London, England, United Kingdom

First Published by Triple Infinity Creations Ltd
First Printing February 2014

BRITISH LIBRARY CATALOGING-IN-PUBLICATION DATA
DOWNER, C.C & LOCKER, A.M.

Paperback ISBN: 978-0-9928334-0-4
eBook-ePub ISBN: 978-0-9928334-1-1
eBook-PDF ISBN: 978-0-9928334-2-8

PUBLISHER'S NOTE
This book is a work of fiction. All of the characters, organisations, and events portrayed in this novel are either products of the author's imagination or are used fictitiously.

Dedication

We dedicate this book to everyone who knows and values their self-worth; to everyone that has forgotten their self-worth; and everyone that is making changes in their lives. Knowing your self-worth and valuing it is important.

Sometimes we take people for granted whether consciously or not, we forget about the feelings of those people.

Remember we only have one life to live; don't take it and the people around you for granted.

Stay true to yourself.

CC & AL

First of all let us thank you for taking the time to indulge in this book. AL and I have been friends for many years and often discuss the difference of opinion when it comes to encounters between the opposite sex. No, this isn't one of those self-help books explaining how to engage in your relationships. Honestly I don't knock those books some of them are very insightful. As a bookworm I've come across many, many books but none of them tell you both sides of the same story, which is where AL and I got the idea to really shed some light on those….what we call "encounters."

2 Sides 2 the Story tells the same story in the opinion of each member of the party. As we all know Men and Women are from two different planets and most of the time have a totally different perspective on situations. This often causes complications. Generally men can separate sex from their emotions, and it is known that women are more emotionally attached to their encounters. Men are more likely to be involved in "no strings attached" relationships e.g. booty calls, friends with benefits, creeping with mistresses and often cannot understand why women are more likely to hold on to the situation.

2 Sides 2 the Story puts some situations in to perspective and may help individuals to consider their actions before they act them out. It goes to show that sometimes what we assume is going on in the minds of the opposite sex; our assumptions are far from the truth.

As you take the time to read through each of these encounters from different groups of people, I truly hope you can laugh, nod and agree or disagree. It would be great if you would voice your opinions and lets us known whether you are male or female and who you agree with or disagree with. Find us on twitter @3icreationsOrg, @ccdowner, @ Alvonne2 and Facebook Triple Infinity Creations

Now we do warn you this book is not for the faint hearted and some scenes can be quite graphic so if your children have access to your books please be warned and put them away.

As always there are *2 Sides to the Story* scrap that there's also the truth. Happy reading!

Contents

Story 1: Tracy & Antoine

Antoine

"Hey Tracy" Adding some bass to my already baritone, I laid the seduction on through the phone.

"Hey Boo! What's good?" Tracy replied cheerily.

"Nothing just sitting here and thought I'd give you a bell." Guys, you know how we always have to make these ladies feel special. I was actually kicking back relaxing on my own; boredom had gotten the better of me. Tracy was probably the fifth or sixth girl I had called today. All my links were busy.

"That's nice of you!" Tracy replied.

I could hear the smile in her voice. "What you doing later?" I asked holding my breath for a second.

"Nothing!" She said excitedly.

"You fancy coming down?" Picturing her eyes lighting up I thought of her full lips on my manhood.

"Ok cool!"

"See you about 9.30." Just like that the conversation ended.

Tracy, Tracy, Tracy....Wow I'm in troubleeee. Tracy is a city banker. We met one day a few years back, when I first opened an investment banking account. I remember it, like it was yesterday. Her eyes popped out of her head when I walked into the bank requesting a meeting with one of their investment bankers. She was sitting behind her desk, in a pinstriped suit, her hair pulled into a tight bun. She had on a pair of glasses that were resting low on the bridge of her nose. Her cat-like eyes and her dimples made my dick hard. We met a few times for lunch to get to know each other better.

One day I just couldn't resist those curves any longer. I pulled her into the stairwell of her bank building and hiked up her skirt, once I realised she had no panties on, I gave her a hot quick screw against the wall. What can I say? That girl's pussy was on fire. She really knew how to work those muscles. Ever since that day I've enjoyed fucking Tracy. The only downfall is I struggle to keep up with her insatiable appetite, plus she talked too much and was trying to catch feelings. I'm not the settling down type. How am I supposed to make all these women happy if I settle with just one?

"Come on Antoine, you know you can handle her." I said to myself as I paced up and down the length of my penthouse preparing for what I knew was going to be a long night. "Fuck it! I'm gonna do me, if she isn't happy after, she can fuck off. I've got many more numbers to dial."

Picking up the magazine that had been delivered this morning, I read the article about my portfolio. "*Professional Athlete, 6'1, with a lean chiselled muscular frame. His intense smoky green eyes will strip you of all inhibitions. Guess what ladies he is single….*" Laughter erupted from deep within my chest as I remembered the journalist, and the way she was ready to pounce on me on during the interview. The photographer had done a good job at the photo shoot; I have to admit I looked HOT. I studied the spread of pictures and the captions. There was a face shot; a picture of me in a crisp white suit; and the pull-out centrefold was a portrait of my naked profile from the back exposing my most recent ink; *Angel wings*. Reclining on the couch, remote in hand I flipped on the recording of my most recent track meet to study my competition, my form and mentally prepare for my next performance.

Two hours later…..

Buzz, buzz! The intercom system rang. "Hello?" I asked cheerily.

"Mr Greene, there's a lady by the name of Tracy here to see you" The concierge spoke softly into the phone.

"Thanks Diana, send her up." Disconnecting the call I looked in the hall mirror and inspected my appearance. I was wearing a grey fitted shirt, with a dark grey pair of Armani jeans, my bare feet were freshly creamed revealing my neat manicured toes; my bald dome shiny; a final squirt of *Invictus* aftershave, and I was ready to satisfy this woman. "Looking good Toine, looking good." I said with a smile to my reflection.

Tracy knocked once before she realised the front door was open. "Hey you, looking good as usual!" Tracy complimented, as she stepped in wearing a red knee length mac, a pair of red thigh high boots.

"Thanks babes." I smiled, kissing her on the cheek. My imagination was running wild; I couldn't wait to see what she wasn't wearing underneath her jacket.

I escorted her into the spare room. Don't shake your head and keep your comments to yourself. The only reason she was even in the penthouse is because I was feeling too lazy to leave the house. Sheeeeit, not every female gets to enter the Master's Playroom where all the magic happens.

We sat on the edge of the bed. "Fancy a drink?" I asked.

"Sure." Her gaze followed my every move.

"What do you fancy?" I queried on route to the bar.

With a seductive look and a pout of her lips she replied "'Toine juice!"

Her answer halted me on the spot. Tracy is one horny female and always willing to please. I laughed. Tracy dropped to her knees, releasing the zip and pulling my lengthening cock from the confinements of my jeans. Her wet lips swallowed me whole taking me straight to the back of her throat.

"Damn Tracy, easy you're going...oooo...to...uh make me ...oooo....cum." I groaned fighting the urge while my eyes rolled back in my head.

"No you won't!" Tracy mumbled, as she continued to work her magic on my pulsating wood. Her deep throat action was second to none. I couldn't believe how good it felt. I felt those first waves of spunk creeping up my dick.

"Aww awe eww shitttttttt!" Unable to hold it back anymore I watched my spunk shoot out all over her face.

I know, I know, what can I say I needed to bust my load and the way her lips worked, it really was an A star for technique and style. Come on guys don't judge me, you have to admit when a blow job is professional your toes will be curling too.

"Are you going to fuck me now babe?" Tracy asked, too calmly. The look on her face implied she was struggling to maintain her niceness.

"Yes babes, just let me get my energy back." I stifled a yawn and attempted to stroke her breast. The look on Tracy's face was scary. Her eyebrows rose off of her face in a scowl; she looked like she wanted to rip me another ass hole. She sat on the edge of the bed, stroking her cunt. My eyelids were heavy; I tried to watch as I lay my head on the pillow with a smile of contentment on my face. The release of weight from my loins was like a drug.

I felt Tracy undo the buttons on my shirt, the warmth of her naked flesh on my chest; she ran her tongue up and down my washboard abs.

"Babe don't tell me you're fucking snoring?" Tracy shouted, poking me in my chest.

"No! Don't be stupid just resting my eyes." I replied half opening one eye and looked at her. Little did she know I was out for the count and had no intentions of rising anytime soon! The last thing I remembered was the sound of the front door slamming shut and Tracy telling me to delete her number. "Fuck you!" I said to the empty apartment. "There are so many willing to take your place. So many more where you came from." I slurred as I passed out.

Tracy

"Hey Max, girl you'd never believe who called me?" I was so excited and couldn't wait to tell my story.

"David? Mark?" Maxine quizzed me, jumping on my excitement.

"Nah Hun, Antoine!"

"Antoine? .....Wow..." Disbelief twanged her voice.

"Yea thick dick, green eyed Antoine! You know the one with the body that will make your mother sing." I chuckled.

"Oh, yeah." She replied.

"So anyway, he's like you wanna come over? I'm like fuck it. Yea I'm on my way. Last time we fucked it wasn't too bad. He's an early racer, but his dick felt right. So after a hot soak, fresh nail polish on my toes, I fixed my hair and got naked under my red mac and fuck me boots."

"Oh shit you went in." She chuckled.

"It's been a while since I've felt a thick dick; my body was in desperate need of some." I explained, I walked into my kitchen and poured myself another glass of Pinot.

"So anyway, two hours later, I'm knocking on his door.

His eyes practically popped out his head."

"Oh yea" Maxine snickered.

"He tried to play it cool. I backed his ass up, dropped his pants. That thick head was bobbing and weaving." I paused for effect and imitated Antoine's actions.

"Ump ummmp ummmm. Damn girl, it's been a while stop teasing me, what happened next?"

I fought to keep the laughter out of my voice. "So I'm giving him a BJ ... less than 5 minutes later..."

"No T, don't tell me!"

"Girl, he's bitching and yelling awww, awww shit I'm cumming! He hit that falsetto" No longer able to maintain my composure I fell out in hysterics. "I'm like WHAT THE FUCK! Ahh hell no! You better hold that shit back. Girl one more lick and he was done. He was shooting his load all over the place!" I couldn't stop laughing as I explained what happened, my sides were hurting so much as the memory of his face twisted and his toes curling played through my mind. I have to admit I am still a bit peeved that I drove all the way to his place and didn't get what I went for.

"Whaaaaaaaaaat! HAHAHAHA, T, you've got to be kidding me. There is no way Mr Superstar Athlete is a minute man?"

"Girl, that's not even the worst of it. I let that slide for a couple minutes. I look over at him, the man's out cold snoring like the orient express. I hadn't even got undressed. I picked up my purse. Told his ass to delete my number and slammed that fucking door." Shaking my head at the memory of Mr Antoine 'I'm a Super Star Athlete' Greene. "Maxine, I was so mad, all now my vajayjay is on fire." Maxine had tears streaking down her face, spilling her wine on the floor in the process of uncontrollable laughter.

"Girl these pretty faces, smooth talking limp dick guys are too busy faking it to make it."

"Then they wonder why we ladies are resorting to battery operated toys."

"Hi-Five!" We clapped our hands high in the air. I walked over to the entertainment unit, turned up the volume and started dancing. Maxine caught on and, we danced till the wine was finished and the music had us exhausted.

Story 2: Flex & Judith

Flex

"Hey babes, what time is your flight?" I sat on the bed and watched as Melinda threw the last of her toiletries into her case.

"Six-thirty." Her barely audible mumble resonated through the en-suite bathroom door.

"Ok, I'll drop you to the station, then I'll come back and relax," I offered, thoughts of peace and quiet with no nagging in my ears. A welcome break indeed.

"Make sure you take care of my flat until I get back." I looked at Melinda with a smile pulling her into my arms and giving her a reassuring hug.

"Don't worry, babes. I've got this!" I put on my most sincere smile. 'Wow, fucking freedom for a week! My girlfriend's flat all to myself. Melinda and I had been together for just over six months. She is a 22 year old air hostess. Her blonde hair, blue eyes and luscious toned body had my soldier ready for action. We met on a flight from Malaga; she served me the sweetest pink pussy on that flight.

The sound of my phone ringing interrupted my thoughts of freedom. "What's up bruv?" I looked over my shoulder to make sure Melinda was not within earshot.

"No a damn thing, I'm just doing my workout."

"Cool. Check this David."

"Bruv stop calling me that ok!" He grumbled.

David *cough, cough* I mean Trey is my boy from way back in the day. He was using his code name, which meant he was in the vicinity of his latest conquest.

'Trey' is a gigolo he has created a career out of having

23

women paying his bills and giving him whatever he wants or needs. I often wonder how he does it; he's not the prettiest grape of the bunch.

"Sorry Trey! What's up?" I apologised.

"You know that girl I'm banging?" He whispered.

"Are you serious bruv, which one?" I replied shaking my head.

"Come on man, you know the African chick."

"Yea, yea, Ms African 'Britain's Next Top wanna be super model.' I know the one. When you gonna let me get a piece?" The African chick had a body that most women paid for. I recalled Trey telling me how she had said her ultimate fantasy was to have a *ménage à trois*. We were more than willing to help these women live out their fantasies especially since they were willing to pay for the service.

"Easy Tiger, that's why I'm calling you." His voice thrummed with excitement.

"For real?" I punched the air excited about the opportunity to get some new pussy.

"For real, what you on later?"

I peeped over my shoulder to make sure I was still alone. "Chilling."

"Cool I'm gonna link up with you about seven and we can go to a bed and breakfast with that piece."

"Nah bruv!"

"What do you mean no?" He exclaimed. I could hear the agitation in his voice.

"Bruv, calm down! Good news, my girl's out for a week I got her keys."

"Lucky git!"

"Yes bruv! I've got her like that!"

"So why didn't you say that?"

"I just did!"

"I'm gone!" Cutting the call I looked at my watch.

"Mel, baby you ready? Let's go or you are going to be late." Picking up her case I walked out the door.

A little after seven my girlfriend's doorbell rang. I quickly got up off the floor after finishing my press ups. A man's got to be pumped, I can't let my boy's body out shine mine. "Yo, come in." I smiled, stepping aside to let David, oops I mean Trey and his lady friend walk in.

"Flex this is Judith, Judith meet Flex." Trey led the way down the hall.

"Nice to meet you Flex." Judith held her hand out for me to shake.

"Hey Judith, can I take your coat?" Judith was a sexy African chick 5'10, mahogany smooth skin, pert little titties, her waist nipped in meeting the top of her long shapely legs. When she turned around to give me her coat, I was introduced to her donkey ass. Nicki Minaj had nothing on Judith. The face wasn't the best to look at, but who gives a damn about her face. I will bag that shit if I had to. It's all about the coochie baby!

After half hour of chit chat trying to be polite I got the shock of my life. Judith declared "Listen I did not come here for small talk are we going to fuck or what?" The look on my face was priceless.

It did not take long before the sounds of sex echoed throughout the room. Sitting on the sofa facing the couple, I watched Judith, Trey was in his zone. Judith sat on his cock riding him. I couldn't help but join in.

Releasing my cock, I took some of Judith's sex juice and massaged her bum hole. Not being too brutal I slowly entered her very tight back door. This girl was no joke, within fifteen minutes of pounding Judith, I heard a loud moan. 'Fuck Trey was done!' As he slipped from under Judith I continued to bang the slut's back door. I rammed that slut so hard my fucking dick was hurting; but there was no way I was going to leave this trick hanging after my boy fucked up. *Bam, bam, bam*! I pounded that ass like my life depended on this pussy. Finally I heard the magic words.

"I'm cumming baby!" She groaned. She was covered with a shiny layer of perspiration.

'Yes!' I smiled to myself, wiping the sweat from my brow. After she released a ground shuddering moan I shot my load into her tight ass.

Judith sat in the chair catching her breath; looking sated, as she rubbed her pussy after the session. Pulling up my jogging bottoms I walked towards the bathroom. It was time to get cleaned up and get these two out of my girl's place.

She stopped me and said, "Can I get your number?"

Fucking slag hell no. I thought to myself the gall of her asking for my number after she's doing my friend. Besides she's nothing but a trick with a hole, the size of Sweden. Turning I walked away.

Judith

Trey kneeled on the floor tongue delving deep, licking and sucking every inch of my juicy peach while massaging his peeny weeny. I locked my thighs round his head, enjoying the pleasure of his tongue's work. For a guy with only 5 inches that was as slim as a finger, the way worked his tongue was truly amazing. My head flew back and, my legs trembled. "Oh Trey, that felt good." Smiling content with himself he stood up, his peeny weeny dripping spunk all over his carpet. I closed my eyes to suppress my laugh. He walked out the room to wash up. I pulled out my pocket rocket and finished what he started.

Five minutes later, he walked back into the room. "J, get up we about to go check my boy." He grunted.

I rolled my eyes and pulled on my denim micro skirt and t-shirt, and a pair of converse and I was ready. I walked into the bathroom; wiped out my fanny, still feeling horny I cocked my foot up on the side of the bath and fingered myself real quick. The banging on the door disturbed my flow. Sighing deeply, I walked out the room, an attitude hitting the ground with every step. "If this dude's hot I'm gonna let him hit it." I muttered to the empty hallway.

I had been spending time with Trey; unfortunately with his little Willy and mediocre face, he really wasn't my type. But he was free with his money. We weren't really in a relationship. It was more an arrangement that suited my needs. Whenever my vagina needed eating he was just one call away. If I called he came running, tongue out and ready to do the work he would leave straight after he ate, unless I asked him to stay for longer, which on occasion, when I was feeling lonely I would do so. We'd had sex twice in the last year. To be honest with you the sex really wasn't worth opening my legs, and he seemed content just eating my vagina. With that said the arrangement stuck. From the day I met him he had been working hard to impress me, with gifts and dinner dates. I think he just enjoyed having me on his arm. Who wouldn't? I'm an African Beauty Queen!

Trey was always willing to take me out and was a great conversationalist. What he lacked in looks, dick and size, he made up for in personality. He was a very creative person. He would send me flowers whenever I went on photo shoots. He would treat me like a queen. When I told him my one true fantasy was to have a threesome, he said he had the man for the job. It's taken me the last year to get the Dutch courage to finally agree to do it.

The drive from Poplar to his friend's place in Docklands took 15 minutes in his beat down Mark II VW Golf, which he called a classic. That thing was so faded with rust patches on the arches. The passenger seat rocked every time we went over a bump. The upholstery was being held together in patches by duct tape. Whenever I asked him why he didn't upgrade he said he has better things to spend his money on. Then he would drop the line. 'It's better than catching the bus.' So I learned to shut my mouth. Especially since at the moment I didn't have my own car. 'Hmmm his dude's got money.' I thought looking at the swanky newly built block of expensive apartments. Smiling to myself I followed Trey out of the car park to the elevator, we rode to the 5ᵗʰ floor in silence. The block was plush. I walked in impressed with what I saw. Inside the apartment was remarkable, and impeccably clean. The open plan kitchen area had marble countertops and the living area had all white furnishings.

His boy Flex looked like he just stepped out the gym wearing a tracksuit, his body was hot, his face was not! I looked him over, the imprint of his lunchbox appeared to be a decent size. It was obvious he thought he was all that. He was strutting around like a peacock sprouting its feathers.

We sat around; I stifled a yawn these guys need to wake up man they were boring. They sat around drinking and playing the Xbox. I may as well get this party started. I pulled peeny weeny out and started stroking. Trey lay back on the end of the corner group. Once peeny was hard, I mounted him. Believe me it didn't take but a minute. Letting Flex see the curves of my ass I leaned forward licking on Trey's neck. I twerked my ass and clapped my cheeks, giving Flex a show. I imagined peeny weeny being 10 inches long and filling me up. Out the corner of my eye I glimpsed Flex rub his chin. I faked a really loud moan.

Trey whispered in my ear. "Baby this pussy is too good."

It took Flex a quick minute to spit on my ass and sink his rod in my tight hole. This time my moan was real. We worked until we found the perfect motion. The friction from Trey's nappy pubes sending erotic pulses up my spine. Flex's cock throbbed in my ass. I shocked myself, this was the first time I had experienced a dick in my ass. I'll be damned the pleasure and pain combination actually felt good. He dug in there like he was going for gold.

Trey grabbed my hips. "Oh shit!" He bit his bottom lip and jerked twice.

Damn, he's over already. Sigh just as it was getting good. Flex shifted me so he could get in deeper, my ass jiggled while he fucked me hard. I played with my fanny pearl till I exploded. "Oooo I'm coming baby." I announced. Wow. That was good. I sat back on the chair. I have to get this dude's number. He can hit this again. He held his dick as he limped out the room. "So can I get your number? We can do this again without your boy?" He kept on walking with no reply. "Forget you too." I muttered. "Your dick weren't all that." I got up fixed my clothes. "Trey I'm ready to go."

"Nah J, I ain't ready." I looked at him semi sedated, with his hand gripping his peeny weeny. Disgusted I picked up my shit; grabbed his car key and walked out the door.

Fifteen minutes later my phone started popping. I laughed to myself. I rejected the call. "Peeny weeny wants to play me. Fuck that." I laughed to myself. The calls came non-stop back to back. I parked up his beat down mobile a few roads from home. I left the keys in the glove box and walked away. I know people may think that I deserved the treatment that I received; it's my own fault for fucking them both but sometimes a woman has needs and if one man can't satisfy them why not try two? Besides if a man can do it, why can't I? As for taking his car, what did you expect me to do? Walk?? Yea right that is hilarious!

Story 3: Tracy & Mark

Mark

"You ready Mate?" I said down the phone.

"Yes, we're ready."

"Cool, I'll meet you fellas in a bit!" I picked up the keys to my V8 and walked out the door. Unlocking the Q7, I powered up that beast and drove down the A13 towards Southend. Within half an hour I had arrived at my destination. "This fucking SUV is going to make me lose my licence." I thought of the speeds that I had been clocking all the way down here. Good thing the roads are empty. I said to myself.

Pulling up alongside an all-white Range Rover, I rolled down the passenger window.

"What's good, blood?" asked Brinks. The driver of the Range had been a long-time friend of mine. We had spent a lot of time together on the Army base after my last tour of Afghanistan a few years back. He had been discharged after getting shot in the hand.

"Same old shit, different day!" I replied.

"I haven't been to Southend in ages. I'm looking to get my mind blown by these Essex girls. You know they love some big cock." Brinks stated.

"What's up player?" Mervyn shouted from the passenger side of the Range.

Mervyn was Brinks' mate but I could not stand to be around the guy for too long. Mervyn was a married man. He has family life but still sleeps around like he is single. I can't stand those fools, either you are in or you are out. Greedy fucker!

The music in the Q7 stopped and a familiar voice came

through the speakers.

"Hey Mark."

"Hey Tracy, how are you?"

"I'm good. What you up too?"

"Just taking a drive with my mates." Sudden silence filled the Q7. "Tracy? Tracy, are you still there?" I shouted looking at the display to see if the call had been disconnected.

"Yes I'm here. Mark take me off speaker please" Her sultry tone called out.

"Ok, one sec." Tracy was a girl I would entertain now and again if we were both free. Tracy had a "Don't give a damn" mentality and that is why we got on. What Tracy wants; Tracy gets no if, buts or maybes.

"Mark?"

"Yes Tracy?"

"Are your friends nice?"

"Why?"

"I'm just asking!"

"Yeah they're ok."

"You wanna come around?" Tracy asked.

"One sec Tracy." After putting her on mute, I turn to my boys in the Range and spring the surprise on them. "Chase pussy or sure pussy?" I asked them after informing them of Tracy's suggestion. It didn't take long for them to make a decision, they jumped into my SUV. I spun the Q7 around at the next junction and headed towards Tracy's house.

Pressing Tracy's buzzer, she immediately let us in. We entered the lift and head to the fourth floor.

"Hey Trace." I called as I entered the flat.

"Hey Mark, I'm upstairs close the door and come up."

We walked up the stairs toward Tracy's room. I could not ignore the smile on Mervyn's face when he saw her. As usual Tracy had set the mood. The dim lights and sweet smell was lovely. Tracy was lying across the bed condoms spread all over the sheets and her dildo, Jack, was in her hands.

I hate Tracy's dildo, the fucking thing was too big and made me insecure. Wasting no time taking my trousers off, I put my dick on those sexy lips. Tracy's wet lips and cool tongue instantly engulfed my cock. I watched Mervyn staring at Tracy's pussy.

"Stupid, are you gonna lick my clit or you just gonna eye fuck it?" Tracy asked.

Dumbfounded Mervyn looked at her in disbelief, hesitated for a second then came to life. Not waiting to be asked a second time Mervyn started eating Tracy's pussy like he was starving.

"Damn homeboy, you starving or something" I chuckled.

Mervyn just looked up and smiled. Brinks rolled on a rubber, pulled Tracy onto all fours and slipped his throbbing dick into Tracy's ass, while Mervyn ate her pussy from underneath her. I observed Tracy work her magic on us. The sight had my cock rock hard as I fucked her deep throat.

Pleasure rippled up the tip of my cock, up my spine and down my toes. Once I bust my first load over her face, I swapped places with Brinks, my cock ready and willing to spread that ass wide open.

Two hours later we were all totally drained, but Tracy seemed like she was just getting warmed up! With exhaustion and contentment spread over everyone's faces, we all got up and left. Within minutes of leaving she rang and asked me to come back for round two. I dropped my boys back to their car "This woman is going to be the death of me, but that pussy was too good to turn down" I said to the empty car.

Hmmm I wonder what my surprise is that she promised me.

Opening the door to Tracy's flat, I heard low female moans. Surprised by the beautiful sight every man fantasizes about I entered the room with the biggest smile on my face. Angel was getting busy on Tracy's clit. "I love these freaks!"

Tracy

I sat listening to some slow jams. The warm glow and sweet aromas of the scented candles lit the room; the ambiance had my body yearning for some attention. I'd been playing with myself for nearly an hour but, just couldn't get satisfied. My phone vibrated the picture of a big pink dick flashed up, *Christina Aguilera's 'Nasty Naughty Boy'* began playing. Smiling I left the phone to ring. Jumping in the shower with thoughts of the fun I was about to have, I prepared myself for a night of fun and frolics. Once I was out the shower; I moisturised my hot sensitive skin with some coconut oil, dabbed Hugo Boss on my delicate areas. Now I can return Mr Big Dick's call. Oblivious to most of the conversation all I heard were the most important words "I'm on my way!" I prepared the room for the evening's entertainment. Sending his photo in a message to my girl-friend with the message simply put "11." We had a special code for situations like this, and I knew she would understand.

Angel and I had been best friends since school. She knew me like I knew myself. Her dark Bambi eyes, long thick black hair and her petite frame made her my opposite. I was tall, athletic with short red hair and hazel eyes. I worked hard, played hard and in between all of that spent much of my time in the gym. When it came down to getting our groove on we were on the same page. We were inseparable. We shopped together; partied together and up until recently we had even worked together. We had put ourselves through university stripping and escorting wealthy individuals. Now we both have high paying jobs in the finance industry. We are women who take control of our situations and live life the way we choose to live it.

Within minutes, the door was knocking. The sounds of confident footsteps climbing the stairs travelled to my play room. The doorway filled with 200lbs of solid sun kissed muscle; I could not help but smile. I eyed Mr Big Dick, aka Mark; his confident grin exposed his dimples. I took my big nipple in my mouth and licked it like a lollipop, my eyes never leaving his. A cough jerked my attention away from him. Stepping into the room, Mark made space allowing me to see behind him. My instant assessment of them was strong, medium, weak. Especially the one they called Mervyn. There's no way that puny boy is ready for me. He looked just like Mr Bean. He looked like he lacked any form of strength. His disposition seemed that of an inexperienced boy in a grown man's body.

I walked naked across the room to Mark, pulled him by his shirt collar and led him to the bed. Allowing them to enjoy my big round ass as it jiggled with each step. I crawled onto bed, twerking my booty as I went along. I heard the collective gasp as I dropped into a full split and shook my ass cheeks. I had been a stripper for many years and knew the tricks to please the crowd.

I saw the expression on their faces, when they saw Jack, my 12inch blue dildo. Laughing to myself, I spread my legs wide and rubbed Jack provocatively on my kitty.

I could not resist a giggle when I saw three crotch tents pop up from the pressure of their hard dicks begging for release. I grabbed Mark's dick knowing how to please him. Working my magic until a moan escaped his lips. Mervyn looked like he was waiting to be spoon fed. Obviously Mark failed to educate his friends about how I get down. "Stupid, you going to lick my clit or you eye it?"

The one named Brinks was licking on my breasts no instructions necessary. I reached in his pants amazed that for a man his size he was packing a long slender mushroom head.

Taking both dicks in my mouth I rolled condoms on them, and double sucked both while Mervyn ate my sweet peach like he was starving. His technique needed a lot of work, his rough tongue applied too much pressure on my vagina; he bit my clit causing me to jump harshly. Frustrated with his immature skills I got on all fours; still sucking on Mark's dick.

Brinks spread my ass cheeks slapping each one making them jiggle. Backing up on him I bounced my ass. He entered me hard, no time for hesitation. "Oooo yeah, give me that cock." I moaned.

Mervyn climbed under me and licked my clit suckling on it, his wiry moustache scratching my lower lips as he inserted his tongue licking my inner walls. Brinks' dick delved deep into the tightness of my ass. Every thrust, lick and plunge they gave me, I hit them back twice as hard. The walls echoed with the sounds of ass clapping, ball slapping pussy munching sex.

The rotation went on for 2 hours. All the men collapsed from exhaustion and multiple climaxes. I walked around the scattered bodies, to retrieve a tall glass of water. I stood looking at them for a while. Mervyn was curled up in a fetal position on the floor. Brinks' dick was pointing towards the sky as he laid spread eagle on the chaise lounge; Mark lay on his side, his arm resting across the empty side of the bed I had just vacated. I could not wait to air out the scent of sex. Before climbing into the shower, I opened the windows. I washed away the sweat, and the spunk.

"Man I still need to explode. Three men and, still no release!" I mumbled into the cascade of water.

By time I got out they were dressed and barely able to walk down the stairs. I laughed as Mervyn stumbled down them. "What's up Merv? Are your legs feeling weak?" I laughed, before closing the door behind them.

Still in the mood for some male company I picked up the phone. "Mark, drop your boys off and come on back lets finish what we started." I smiled before hanging up. I walked back upstairs and changed the sheets before lying down.

I woke up to a wet tongue travelling up and down my legs and ass. Moaning I spread my legs further. "Oooo" keeping my eyes closed I felt soft fingers slip into my moistness. Turning me over, I waited with anticipation. I felt the curvaceous soft mounds travel up my thighs. Her skin felt like soft silk, the smell of cocoa butter and Dior wafted up my nose.

I felt the delicate feel of my girl's tongue followed by her breasts, travelling up my body as she mounted me. I moaned the pleasurable feel of Jack filling my walls. My body covered in droplets of lust filled sweat. Arching my back for maximum depth; pawing her breasts and stroking her nipples, I adjusted myself. I felt another pair of hands on my legs spreading my legs wider.

I heard Mark's delightful moan. I watched him enter Angel's lips, her tongue circling his thick dick. I looked up, smiling. With his wet dick, he entered Angel's pussy from behind. His thrust made her sink deeper inside me. She groaned with pleasure, as did I. Her breasts rubbed mine, her tongue danced a familiar dance with my own. Mark wrapped his arms round our waists, fucking Angel hard so she could fuck me harder.

"Fuck us baby, take these pussies" Angel demanded.

The fuck fest went on till the early hours. Our bodies dripped with sweat. Shattered on my seventh orgasm, I cried out passionately. Mark and Angel fucked me so good. With a final thrust, we all collapsed in a heap, both of them inside of me. We fell asleep.

Story 4: Stacey & Tom

Tom

"The girls on these porn movies are so hot, some guys are so lucky. I can't stand these muscle bound porn stars. They are always some ugly fuckers that seem to get the sexiest girls in these movies." Disgruntled and horny I stroked my dick with my left hand; imagining myself smashing both these ladies within inches of their lives. "I'm horny! Fuck me dammit." I said to the imaginary women stroking my cock. I was about to release my load when there was a sharp knock on my door. "You must be kidding me not now." I muttered.

I lay on the couch with the DVD on mute, hoping that the intruder would go away. *Knock, knock!* The person knocked harder. "For fuck sake! Ugh!!" Pulling up my shorts, I walked to the door thinking to myself, 'this better be an emergency'. I cracked the door to see who was getting between me and my nut, my prayers were answered.

"Hey Tom!" The pretty redhead, with her cat-like green eyes stood twisting her hands nervously hopping from one foot to another.

"Hey Stacey, can I help you?" Stacey was my next door neighbour. She moved in with her man, a few weeks prior.

I watch her every morning as she gets into her car to go to work, or when she goes for a run in the afternoon. She spends a lot of time in my dreams. Stacey is hot! The first day they moved in next door we had a brief chat, unfortunately, that was the only time we had spoken.

"Tom, sorry to bother you but I've locked myself out

of the apartment by mistake any chance I can go across your balcony to let myself back in. That door is always open." Stacey was standing in the passage with just a towel wrapped around her.

"How did you get locked out Stacey?" I asked in an attempt to prolong the conversation, she had my soldier at attention.

"I just came out to pick up my mail and the door slammed shut." A big smile came to my face, but I played it cool. I knew she was lying because these doors can only be locked by using a key.

"Sure Stacey, no problem. Come on in!"

She walked into my flat, her hips swaying sensually, speaking a language directly to my manhood. I just knew my prayers were answered; I could feel her eyes travelling up and down my half naked body.

I had pictured fucking Stacey more than a few times in the last couple of weeks, and now here she is in my flat wearing a towel. I wonder if she's naked underneath.

"Let me open the back door for you" I offered, leading the way into the living room.

"Huh" Stacey's gasp caused me to spin.

"Is anyth…" I saw Stacey's face turn beet red, I guess the image of a woman spread wide with two dicks in her, on a 50inch TV screen would be a shock to anyone. I searched for the TV remote to turn it off.

The tug on my dick from behind caused an instant resurrection. I turned around Stacey's towel was on the floor, and she was stark naked in front of me. Her pert firm breasts, and soft flat stomach sent a sudden shiver through my body. Blinking repeatedly, I had to confirm I wasn't dreaming. I tried to speak but the words would not come out, perfection was the only word I can find to describe this angel standing in my apartment. Stacey was five feet six with a bottle shaped body big ass small waist and tits to die for all wrapped up in clear silky smooth skin, she had the perfect package. Uncertainty flashed quickly across her face, before she took a step toward me. I became nervous.

"Man up Tom, this cunt is yours." I muttered. Her confidence aroused me.

Stacey wasted no time she grabbed my dick and gave me the head job of a life time. I'm not a selfish guy, so I had to return the favour. Positioning us into a 69, I slowly sucked on her clit she began to moan her juices were dripping, and her bum hole was pulsating around my finger in her ass. Stacey rolled me onto my back and began to ride me like a stallion.

"This pussy is good." Her constant jockeying thrust my cock deep into her walls. My toes curled, my fingers kneading her breasts, pulling her nipples into my mouth, she moaned. Encouraged, I flipped her over hard; her back hit the floor, with a thud.

"Ouch" she cried, her legs wrapped round my waist, plunging deep thrusts knocking out her back wall. Her screams of pleasure echoed throughout the room. Her nails dug deep into my shoulders.

I grabbed her wrists, restraining her arms behind her back. I used my thick dick to slap her face, before forcing my dick in her mouth again. She sucked me hungrily. Her teeth scrapped my cock. I rammed it down her throat she gagged. Tears came to her eyes. My legs buckled as she sucked me like a vacuum. I released her arms. She climbed on top of me and rode me hard. I flipped her again, putting her legs on my shoulders and fucked that pussy. It felt so good and tight. Her walls contracting round my cock.

It didn't take long before Stacey was screaming; her pussy walls clenched then soaked my dick. I knew it was over. Stacey pushed me off of her. I witnessed my first real life woman, squirting in action. I was fascinated by the way she was squirting all over me and the floor. Stacey jumped up, flustered, and rosy cheeked dashing straight back out the door into her flat.

Slightly dismayed I sat up. "Did that really happen?" I looked around reality hitting me. She had fucked me and walked out.

That was the last time I spoke to that girl. That was weeks ago, I saw her around a few times, and she never even made eye contact. Bitch! I felt used again.

Stacey

I walked around my apartment unsure of what to do with myself. I was feeling haunted and unable to settle. Mike had not made love to me in weeks, and he was dead set against me having any sex toys. The need to be free guided me onto the balcony.

"What a lovely day!" I admired the view of the landscaped communal garden. The glow of the sun on my freshly showered skin dried the beads of water, as they rolled off my shoulders down my back.

"What's that noise?" I listened trying to make out what I could hear, the sounds of cheeks slapping and pleasure groans filled the air. I stood listening. I found myself, rubbing my little lady against the towel. I leaned over the balcony to see if I could establish where the noise was coming from.

Still touching myself I walked along the balcony to the left and leaned over seeing nothing. My arousal had me in a trance; I walked to the right, my neighbour. "What's his name? Ahh, Tommy boy!" Like so many of my neighbours, had no curtains and his balcony door was wide open. I watched him sitting on his couch, stroking what looked like a tree branch in his hand. My lips began to water, mesmerised I couldn't take my eyes off him. My fingers worked over time, as slow moans evaded my tongue. My fingers were not enough the fire in me demanded a hose to put it out.

Tom was a weird man. He seemed to be a loner; I had never seen him with a woman. He never had any friends come to visit. I had caught him looking at me on several occasions. At first it had creeped me out, but I just put it down to him being a loner.

Without further thought I was knocking on his door. The noises from the TV had stopped. I pictured him with that branch sitting there. I knocked again, hoping he would hurry up and open the door before I lost my confidence. Finally, he came to the door. My eyes travelled and lingered on his branch that was obviously struggling against the material of his shorts

I don't know what happened next. All I remember is that wood deep in my womb, oh my I had never felt dick like that before. He felt so damn good. He was working me like a pro. My eyes were closed, if only Mike would hit it like this. Every now and again I would look at the huge TV the three were fucking hard. I felt like one of those girls, damn this guy was working me. Before long I exploded all over that dick, my juices shot out across the floor. Shit, I was so embarrassed, I ran back to my apartment barely able to cover myself with my towel.

"Oh no oh no... What just happened?" I cried in the shower I washed away his scent. My little lady was sore from that good wood. I used the shower to ease my soreness. I didn't realise I was in the shower so long.

"Stace where are you? I got a surprise for you!"

"Oooo shit..." I muttered. It took me a while to answer. "Mike I'm in the shower. What's up?" I shouted. I waited for a reply still massaging my little lady. My nipples began to tingle. With my head against the cool tiles, I waited.

2 Sides 2 the Story

I felt a draft as Mike opened the shower screen and stepped in. His tongue travelled up my neck. His dick separated my cheeks as he entered me from behind. Is this guy for real? He hasn't touched me in forever and, then he just sticks his dick inside of me. No foreplay. He humped me for a few minutes, before the sounds resembling a bear having a heart attack filled the room. He quickly pulled out and I felt the hot splatters on my back. I tried to contain my sigh; keeping my back to him silent tears fell from my eye. Is this really worth it? I thought.

A few weeks went by, I was still spying Tommy boy watching his porn. Sometimes he would catch me watching and I would fleet back inside still embarrassed that I had squirted across his floor. I still touched myself to the memory of his wood. Maybe one day I will get up the courage to say hi, again.

Story 5: Roy & Desire

Desire

Being single is no joke in today's climate. The standards of men are lacking in areas; fortunately for me I was young, wealthy and as pretty as they come.

It was a chilly day as I walked along the pier, watching the tide come in. Sitting on the pier, listening to the soothing sound of the water crashing against the shore had become my weekly routine for the past few months. I smiled as I watched him swim into the beach. His strokes were strong against the tide. This was the best part of it. Every Thursday he was there swimming. I had yet to pluck up the courage to talk to him.

Dripping wet and wearing just a small pair of speedos; his athletic body screamed for me to touch it.

I stood watching him as he dried himself off with a towel. He looked my way. We made eye contact for the first time. We smiled; his eyes lit up. I felt like a Cheshire cat. His smile was like an energy field pulling me in his direction. Within seconds, I was just a few metres away from him. I inhaled slowly, and exhaled catching my bearings, my legs floated across the sand. I couldn't believe I was this close. He was taller than I realised, at least 6'2 with a swimmers body. Every breath he took his ripped abdomen moved. This guy looked amazing.

"Why, hello there?" His voice had a thick foreign accent. Just those three words had me creaming in my panties. My brain and mouth had ceased to function, all words had escaped me. My attempt to say something witty and smart vanished; my mind went blank, the cause of which was the movement of his pectorals, every time his arms moved to dry his hair.

"Hi! How was the water?" I finally managed. I was totally distracted by the bulge that was developing in his speedo. The beach was empty as I closed the distance between us.

No rational thought existed, I was fluid motion. I pushed him backwards on the sand. Pulled down his speedos and had his tool in my hand stroking it until it was bouncing out of my hand. I guided it up my skirt revealing my naked crotch. His thick head rubbed against my pearl until it was rock hard. His lips found mine for a deep, butterfly awakening kiss. He held my hips and glided deep inside me. I rode his manhood like a jockey trying to win the Grand National. His fingers played with my pert breasts. Our bodies quivering with heat and a yearning desire to release.

The sex was hot and heated. We rolled around in the sand until I climaxed more times than I could keep track. This man was an athletic beast. He twisted me into positions that I didn't know existed, right there on the shoreline. Damn! Exhaustion and night fall ended our games.

The entire episode had us quivering and panting. We were barely able to stand on our shaky legs. We exchanged numbers on the stroll to my car.

"Excuse me miss, we are about to lock the gates on the pier." The security guard stood watching me.

"Oh thanks." I said quickly gathering up my belongings off the bench next to me. Slightly flustered, I couldn't believe I had been caught daydreaming. I stepped off the pier and walked along the pavement towards home, still in my own world. Bump!

"Oops, oh excuse me!" A gentle voice said. It belonged to the man who stepped out the shop into me. Looking up I realised it was him.

Blushing and flustered I managed to conjure the words "No worries, it's my fault!" My dazed expression travelled with him as he smiled and walked away.

Roy

"Dom, tell me something. Who is that girl, whom sits on the pier every Thursday reading?" Curiosity had the better of me I had been watching this beautiful lady for months. She always sat alone on the pier.

"Man, that's that girl, Desire Jeffery. We went school together, but I doubt she'll remember me. She is Upper class! You know the type!"

Dominic and I had been friends after meeting on the basketball court a few years. We had become good friends.

"Yea I do but every class has a teacher, amigo!" I laughed.

"I feel you, son." He replied looking towards the deserted pier I had been gazing at.

"Dom, I'm out I will shout you later."

"Alright Roy take it easy." Parting ways I walked to my car unable to stop thinking about Desire. I knew deep down one way or another I was going to get her. It's just a matter of time. Judging by the way she was constantly eyeing me up, whenever I get under the shower tap, I knew eventually our time will come.

The need to find out more about this girl prevailed. I sat at my desk and log into my laptop. I type her name into Google she was the first to come up.

"Damn," I whistled.

"Desire Jeffery you, girl must be something special!" I read her Wikipedia profile I was very impressed with her. Youngest ever black CEO of her company at 25 graduated first in her class at Oxford and the list went on. I spent a little longer doing some research, page after page, article after article, I finally found what I was looking for. Desire was recently single, she broke up from her basketball playing, millionaire boyfriend about three months prior, due to his philandering ways. He had cheated on her with some young groupies. The articles stated that he had attempted to rekindle their relationship after she found out about his indiscretions. He went as far as buying her an Aston Martin, it was reported she set it on fire in front of him. As a result charges were filed against him for breaking her nose.

"Fuck I've got some big shoes to fill. I'm going to impress this female one way or the other." I caught myself stroking my chin considering the best way to approach this beautiful girl. I obviously had her attention I just needed to make sure I maintained it. Desire deserved to receive my A-game. Women of her stature would settle for only the best. I would have to step up to the plate and hit a home run. Most girls I managed to impress with my car, or my fancy clothes, or my body but I knew I had to come correct with Desire. This is the type of girl that will shut you down if you approach her in the wrong way. So I had to let her approach me, the major question is: how I should play this?

I knew Desire's Thursday routine like the back of my hand. I had noticed she always fell asleep. Those romantic novels she read must be pretty boring. I had already set the bait, now I just needed to wait patiently since I bumped into her, in the process I had dropped my business card into her open bag.

Two days had passed before my phone rang.

"Good afternoon?" Not recognising the number, accordingly I announced myself professionally.

"Hi!" A soft voice said on the other end of the phone.

"Good afternoon, Roy speaking how may I help you?"

"Hi, umm I'm trying to find a personal training and was recommended to you by a friend." Playing it cool and not blowing my cover, I arranged an induction for Saturday at seven. It was only Thursday and the next two days felt like a life time.

Saturday evening....

By six-thirty I was fresh, clean and ready for the next step in my plan. At minutes to seven, the intercom notified me of her arrival. Her entrance into my private gym, at the back of my house was entrancing. Her aromas flitted around the entire room. She was absolutely intoxicating.

"Good afternoon Miss, I'm Roy." I reached out to shake her hand, smiling at her.

"Pleased to meet you Roy, please call me Desire."

She took in her surroundings before her eyes met mine again. She held my gaze for a long time, sizing me up, eventually losing her confidence; she coyly looked away, fidgeting with the strings on her sweater.

"So...what's your goal Miss Desire? You seem to be in perfect shape at present. How may I assist you?" I watched as she circled the room, stopping directly in front of me.

"Roy let's cut the crap now."

"What do you mean Miss?" Her eyes roamed my body. She reached out and ran her hand down my abs. Her words said one thing, but the look in her eye gave me the impression that she was in a daze.

"I'm in your space now what are you gonna do? I wanna fuck!"

The tone of her voice sent shivers through my body her confidence and natural aura made me nervous but I wasn't prepared to show it. It felt like all the blood was sucked from my head to my manhood. I stood there looking at Desire, lost for words. The silence filled the room. We stood a few feet away from each other observing, digesting, and strategizing internally the next action.

I took the lead in this tango, and stepped towards Desire. She opened her mouth to speak but it was too late, the game was on. I placed my big hand over her mouth and instructed her to zip it.

"I'm your teacher you are my student, so do as your fucking told." The words flew out my mouth I was stunned that she didn't slap me, but she was obedient. "I'm going to fuck you right now! Whatever you do, no matter how you feel, do not touch me!" I could tell by Desire's stunned expression she was not someone used to being told what to do. I will give her credit she played along.

I stripped her naked deliberately teasing her; avidly caressing her shoulders and neck. Calculatingly, I removed her bra with a slow single snap before discarding it amongst the pile already on the floor behind us. Circling her body, I leisurely tweaked her erect nipples between my thumb and forefinger; toying with them until I heard her purr, licking them one by one agonisingly gently.

"Close your eyes." I commanded. Placing my finger on her lips, her tongue darted out to meet it.

Retrieving an ice cube from the freezer, I began to tease Desire. First I rubbed the ice on her erect nipples, then down the back and side of her neck. I enjoyed the way she quivered under my touch. Using the weight of my hands, I applied pressure on her shoulders until she reclined onto the mat beneath her feet. She lay on her back. Spreading her thighs I couldn't resist a smile when I saw her huge fat pussy dripping with her nectar.

Inserting the ice cube in my mouth, I blew the cool air unto her oversized clit making sure not to touch her. Desire's moans were too much for my dick. He was pulsating in my joggers begging to be let free. *Easy boy! We will get there soon.* I said to my dick.

Teasing Desire with ice cubes had her begging for more. I began sucking on her clitoris making sure the cool breeze tantalised her with pleasure. Desire began to shake and I knew it wouldn't be too long before she exploded all over my face. She began vibrating like a washing machine ready to spin her load. I stopped suddenly.

"Why did you stop?" She panted trying to catch her breath a confused expression all over her face.

I looked at her and said "You fucking touched me! Do as you are told!"

"Oh!" Feigning obedience she removed her hands and placed them above her head.

I had to admit to myself I was very impressed with her. Her facial expressions were delightful.

Desire

At first I wasn't sure if I would play along with this little game, but something about this man really drove me into a hot zone. Obediently I lay naked and dumbfounded. Was this guy really talking to me? Does he know who I am? Obviously he feels in charge. Okay every dog has his day. Let him do his thing and I will see how good he can play.

I cannot deny his tongue was sensational. Well it was until he stopped.

"Ok fine! I apologise I won't touch you again." He looked at me contemplating his next step, chewing his bottom lip. *Hmmm, that is so sexy!* Without warning he grabbed my hand and pulled me towards a bench press.

"Lay down with your legs spread wide, on the edge so your ass is hanging off." I looked from him to the bench and back again. He just stood there. His authority was wafting off him in waves of confidence. He looked so sexy with his arms crossed against his gloriously wide chest. "Fuck it." Exhaling I conformed to his instructions with a roll of my eyes at his expressionless face. He covered my eyes with a blindfold he pulled from his pocket. Not knowing what to expect, I lay there. I felt my arms being raised above my head. Then I felt soft silky material being pulled and tightened around my wrists.

"Oooo!" I whispered barely breathing unsure of what was next.

Next he tied my thighs wide open. "What the...?" I felt a warm sensation drizzle down my stomach to my pubis down my slit. "Oooo, oooo" I crooned the dripping felt so sensual. Then everything went quiet. I tried to move it was too quiet I couldn't even hear him breathe. I waited anticipating what was going to happen next.

"Open your mouth!" Slow uncertainty filled my head. "Don't worry; I'm not going to hurt you." His reassurance enabled me to relax and open my mouth. He put something cold and hard in my mouth simultaneously plunging something hot and hard between my lower lips. Toying with my body, the friction on my clit brought me close to climax then he stopped again. "What?" I cried with anticipation and frustration.

"You moaned."

"Humph" I sighed. *This game is starting to bore me,* I thought. No sooner than the thought entered my mind his lips sucked my nipples, then his dick slipped between my vagina walls, momentarily withdrawing to circle my cunt. He didn't stop till I squirted over his washboard stomach. He pulled the cold ball out my mouth, and his dick from my pussy. Yearning filled my empty space. He mounted my face with his dick and bent over and ate my snatch; simultaneously slipping the cold thing in and out.

He licked, sucked and fucked my mouth, my pussy and my ass filling my holes with his dick; plus hot and cold objects. His persistent hole filling made me gag, nevertheless the heat liquefied me. I was so turned on I squirted all over him. I felt his cock begin to pulse on my tongue, releasing the salty taste of his spunk. Then a load shot down my throat so fast I nearly choked. Sighing with contentment he lay there exhausted. I was spent! The slightest brush of his skin against mine, sent tremors through my spine.

What could I say? This man worked me like I had never been worked before. We dozed off. When I woke he led me to the shower, where he washed me so tenderly. I had to admit, I liked his style.

Story 6: Patrick & Mandy

Patrick

"Patrick, Patrick!"

"Yes? What you calling me like that for?" I grumbled sleepily.

"I'm going home."

"Ok babes, speak to you soon." I mumbled through the sheets. Damn I thought she would never leave; pretending to be tired and falling asleep Stacey finally got the message to go. Some girls just don't know when their welcome is up.

Reaching across to the bedside cabinet, I retrieved my iPad. I realised I had new messages in my inbox.

Hi Patrick, sorry I took so long to respond to your message but I'm not on this web site very often.

Mandy finally responded to my message I sent to her over a week ago.

Hi Mandy, don't be sorry I'm not really on the site often myself so I do understand where you are coming from no problem.

I quickly typed my response and hit the send button. The lies I told women. I was on the dating site every chance I got sending emails and responding to others, it was a big part of my everyday routine.

Ping! *Patrick I'm not a big fan of this email stuff if you give me your number we can have a quick chat.*

Mandy's reply came through almost instantly. Wow! This girl seems like she is serious and I'm always game for a chat.

Half an hour later my phone rang. She took her time, keeping a man waiting who does she think she is?

"Hi Patrick" Her voice wasn't what I had expected; it was quite husky for a female.

"Hey Mandy."

"Sorry I took so long, I was just trying to finish up on a report."

"Not a problem, honestly I didn't think you would ring this evening. So...Mandy I guess you're still studying?"

"No, no darling! I wish I'm a teacher. I was just finishing some work stuff. What's your excuse for being up so late Patrick?" She giggled.

A teacher, what a sexy teacher she makes. It's a good thing I'm not still in school, I wouldn't be learning a damn thing. I chuckled to myself.

"Well I just came back from a long haul flight from Jamaica this morning. So I'm still getting used to the time difference."

"Jamaica, how nice I would love to go there one day." Trying to change the topic I quickly asked her about her day. Starting a topic about Jamaica was not a good idea due to the fact I'd never been there. I was only trying to impress her.

Keeping the topic on her, since most women love to talk about themselves, it should be quite easy to distract her from my so called "travels."

"My day was fine loads of lectures and meetings nothing special."

"Tell me, Mandy what's a lovely girl like you doing on a dating site? I would have thought any man who laid eyes on you, would snatch you up in a second." Sugar coating and exaggerating was the best way to get a bit of ass.

"Aww, that's sweet of you to say. Well Patrick, a friend of mine was the one who set up this profile for me. I was in a long term relationship, but we decided to a break for a while. It's been a year now, and my girl-friend decided it was time for me to get back on the dating scene, or as she puts it 'dust off the cobwebs before dementia sets in'. You are the first guy I've actually spoken to on here." I believed Mandy since she had rang me after our first email exchange. I knew she could not be familiar with the rules of online dating. You can't let strange men have your number they could be anybody. I thought to myself.

The conversation with Mandy was truly mind inspiring, she was an experienced cultured woman. A woman who obviously knew what she wanted in life. By the sounds of it, she had made things happen.

After speaking to Mandy for a few hours, I told her I had to get to bed. We arranged to meet the next day for a quick drink.

Mandy's pictures did not pay her any justice. She was five foot four, smooth skin with perfect olive-shaped eyes, with shoulder length naturally wavy hair. Her body was firm and curvy in all the right places. Her makeup was minimal. Her French manicured finger nails were fresh and not too long. I spied her toes those too were perfectly shaped. The toes are the deal sealer for me, if a girl has bad toes it's a major turn off I don't give a monkey's uncle how good looking she is. I am hot stepping it right out of the establishment.

We met at Chicago's a bar, not too far from my place but far enough from hers. "Excuse me Mandy, I need to take this call." Retrieving the vibrating iPhone from my

2 Sides 2 the Story

pocket, turning around I walked to the main entrance "What's good Dre?" I answered, my eyes roaming through the crowd.

"Yo P, where you are you?" The caller asked.

"I'm over at Chicago's, having a drink with this chick."

"Oh yeaaaaaa, do you need that SOS call?" Dre chuckled.

"D, I will keep you posted, you know the drill. Anyway let me get back in there."

"Alright, later!"

After ending the call with Dre I walked back inside looking for Mandy, she waved from a table across the bar. Smiling I waved back and manoeuvred around the dancing patrons. I sat down just as a waitress appeared.

"Can I take your order?"

I looked up and saw Tanya, she raised her eyebrows and looked backward and forward between Mandy and I. Tanya was a girl I slept with on and off. She was a pretty redbone girl but had the brains of a mouse. I give her this she was loyal and gave good head. The look in her eye said that if I didn't get us out of here soon she would cause some trouble.

"Hmm no thanks, we are just leaving" I said motioning for Mandy to get up with me.

Mandy looked at me with questioning eyes, then it was like a light bulb went off in her head.

"I assume we are leaving because of her. Is she your girlfriend or something?"

"Hmm more like a stalker" I muttered. "Do you mind if we go somewhere else and continue to enjoy each other's company, and get to know each other a little better?" I could tell she was enjoying my company and didn't want to part ways.

"As long as wherever we go you won't drag me out because of a 'stalker.'" She laughed.

I felt a blush rise to my cheeks and I laughed with her. "Well, we have two options, your place or mine?"

She chewed her lip contemplating my suggestion. "Well I don't mind another drink, and honestly getting out of this chill. My place is about 40 minutes' drive from here."

"Oh ok, mine is just a quick 10 minute walk." I said.

"I guess it's your place then, lead the way." She replied, she linked her arm through mine. I couldn't help keep the extra pep out of my step. 'Yes my plan is working.' I thought.

Midway through the conversation, I mentioned "We are almost here." I said. My phone began to chirp again.

"By the way my friend Dre has been staying at my place for a few days now. He had a fight with his girl. He and his girl have sorted things out and he has to go home, unfortunately, he has the keys to my flat. I have to go meet him quickly. I'm happy to take you home right after. I hope you don't mind walking to my car?" Facing away from Mandy in order to cross the quiet deserted road I had the biggest smile on my face. My plans are in full motion. Mandy didn't seem like the type of woman that would give up the sex very easily, so I had to formulate a game plan to get with her and my boy Dre was on board to help.

We walked past a late night Off Licence I turned to Mandy and asked "May I get you a drink? It's the least I can do for the disturbance of our evening."

"Ummm...some sweet white wine." She replied.

"Sure, no problem. Would you like anything else while we are in here?"

"Thanks. Hmmm, no I can't think of anything!" We

mulled over the wine selection finally deciding on a bottle of Chardonnay.

Forty-five minutes later we were sitting on the couch in front of the blank TV screen, the drive over had been full of laughter. Mandy seemed to be a really nice lady.

"Are you in a rush to get back home? If not we can maybe… mmm… enjoy the rest of our date, maybe watch a movie or listen to some music or something?" Mandy became more talkative and a bit more comfortable after her second glass of wine. To be honest so was I. I could feel the warmth of the alcohol slurring my words. I'm not much of a wine drinker. It makes me woozy.

"Would you like to dance?" I asked the music was playing soft in the background and the lights were set low creating a relaxing environment.

Mandy wrapped her hands around me. "We can…" I pulled back and adjusted myself.

"Can we? You leaving it like that?" Mandy said looking at me defensively.

"No… We not finished yet" her sigh of relief boosted my head. This one is in the bag. I thought to myself.

"Don't stress." I laughed.

"Oh I'm not stressing! What ya tinkin?" The wine had obviously taken away the superior sophisticated lady, now she was exhibiting signs of a relaxed, round the way girl, etiquette was out the window.

"So far so good, let's see where you're going with it." I held her in my arms slow dancing around the room.

"Cool." She whispered into my neck.

I spun her around and she giggled as she nearly toppled over the coffee table. Catching her quickly and pulling her back into my arms. I looked down into her eyes.

"What's happenin' for the rest of the night" The effects of the wine ignited in our bodies. The look of seduction in her eyes oh and her heated breath on my neck made it difficult to keep my hands from travelling up her curves.

"Jus doin' a few bits, it's coming! Patience" I said as I felt my hood rise again, not knowing what we were talking about I struggled to make any sense.

"Okay." Our bodies moved to the music. Her perfume was lovely and I could tell it was expensive, not the shit most girls wore, like I said I'm all about the details.

We slow danced to the music. Mandy was resting her head on my shoulder. It was time to test the waters and see where this night was going. I found myself groping her handful of breasts. I attempted to reduce my clumsiness although the intoxication of both her body rubbing against mine and the alcohol was making it extremely difficult to concentrate. The close rubbing against each other was causing my love muscle to get hard and I knew Mandy could feel it.

"I'm very sorry; it has a mind of its own."

"Don't be" she replied.

"If it didn't get hard, I'd be more upset."

"What do you mean?" She smiled and rested her head back on my shoulder.

Once the music on the CD player had stopped she removed her head from my shoulder. We both made eye contact again. Not one to waste time and lose the moment I went for it. Mandy's lips were soft and her breath was a combination of minty fresh and wine, the kiss went on for ages and it felt like we became one person.

I had a warm weird feeling inside, I really liked this girl. I think she might be the one, the perfect package I've been trying to find. She took me by surprise when she started to undo my jeans. I was about to ask Mandy if she was sure, she knew what she was doing but she placed her finger on my lips and told me not to stop.

Mandy's lips on my dick were warm and soft sending shivers down my back. Mandy seemed like such a naïve and inexperienced woman, the way she had diverted any attempt I had made to have a sexual conversation. Shocked by her actions and the wet warmth of mouth on my cock had me feeling delirious. The way she massaged my balls with one hand, and the other yanking my shaft was new to me. I have had a few head jobs in my time but this girl was good. I knew I would be unable to hold back, if Mandy continued working her magic. I lifted her up and placed her against the wall. There was no time to take any clothes off. I pushed her panties to the side and fucked her standing up. The passion I felt with this girl was like no other. Is this girl the one for me?

A week had passed since Mandy and I spent that lovely night together, yet I was unable to get hold of her. Just when I was ready to give up an email notification caught my attention. I read the email I could have killed myself. The hurt I felt reading this email was just too much.

Dearest Patrick, The day after we spent our night of passion together my ex-fiancé came back into my life. He has swept me off my feet and apologised for the breakdown in communication. I'm sorry but please delete my number. Mandy. PS thanks for the screw it was nice.

Mandy

"Why do I do this to myself?" I sat flicking through my various profiles from Myspace to Plenty of Fish. My vagina was feeling neglected and so was my mind. It had been nearly a year since I had last had any sex, and the urges were becoming unbearable.

Sigh. "Dead, dead, dead! Hold up who's that?" I noticed the message icon flashing on my Black Planet page.

Hey beautiful lady, I saw your smile it lit up my world just like the sunrise after a stormy night. With that said I thought I should drop you a line.

That is so corny. But he's kind of cute. "Hey Lyrical P, sorry for the delay... nah that doesn't sound right." I pressed the delete button. "Hi Patrick...." Hitting the send button pushing a way from my desk I grabbed a glass of wine curled up on the couch with *Rayven Skyy's Rumble in VA*. Just as I started to get comfy, I heard the message notification on my pc. Quickly checking my mail, I smiled Patrick had replied. Going back to my book and my wine I continued to finish the chapter, the book was getting sooo good. I had to take my hat off to Rayven Skyy, she really knew how to create drama in her writing.

Looking up from my book, I realised half an hour had passed. "Oops" I giggled to myself. Dialling his number he picked up on the first ring.

"Hello" 'Someone's eager' I thought to myself.

"Hi, this is Mandy, is that Patrick?" His voice was slightly high pitched for a guy. Only half listening he seemed to be a bit full of himself. Let's see what he's got to say. We proceeded to line up a date.

A couple hours later the conversation was flowing and

he seemed like a decentish person.

"Anyway, P I gotta go, I umm need to go to bed." I yawned.

"Ok Mandy it was nice talking to you, good night."

"Bye!" Guess what vagina? We may have lined us up a little something, something for tomorrow night. Massaging my clit I brought myself to climax before falling asleep.

"What you doing tonight Mandy?"

"Tam I got a date with some guy that I met on-line." I replied.

"Really? What's he saying?" My friend sounded really surprised, she didn't agree with online dating.

"We are meeting at some bar in his area."

Tam and I had been friends for years. We knew what time it is when it came to men. Never let them know where you live. Never give them your real information, only feed them snippets from your real life. We weren't the settling down type of girls, and had often been told that we had too much of the male testosterone in us. We honestly couldn't handle the heartbreak again so we did what needed to be done, in order to get the release our horny vagina's required.

"Girl be nice is all am saying."

"Hmmm, ummmm." We both burst into hysterical laughter.

"T, you know I'm gonna be on my best behaviour." I chuckled, my voice dipped in sarcasm.

"Oh boy; the poor guy! Girl, please don't kill the people dem pickney." Tam laughed.

"Girl, please?! I'm out, I gotta go get ready." Chucking my phone in my purse, I took one more look in the mirror. "Hot like fire."

I was dressed in a bold red body con dress; all my thick size 18 curves packed into my little dress. My thick legs were wrapped in lace up the calf silver stiletto sandals. Switching off the light I grabbed my keys and walked out the door. I waited a few minutes for my cab to arrive.

I wonder if he looks the same way he does in the picture. The 20 minute car journey flew by, my mind filled with memories of the last guy I met online. Alex was a black dude in a white guy's body. He used borrowed pictures on his profile. Sigh. "Driver, pull up on the corner please." Taking a deep breath I stepped out the cab.

I walked into the bar looking around. The bar had a mixed crowd, mostly females as usual. I began walking towards the bar, I spotted Patrick. He looked skinnier in person than he did in the pictures. He had on dark jeans, black V-neck t-shirt which fit his trim shape nicely. He was so engrossed in a conversation with a skinny light skinned chick that he didn't notice me walking up behind him. "Ah hell nah!" The audacity of this man, about he's talking to another woman while he's waiting for me. I squeezed between the two of them.

"Excuse me!" I said ever so sweetly to Patrick while giving the light skinned skinny chick the look to let her know what time it is. I turned and smiled at Patrick. "Hey P, how are you doing boo?" I sealed it with a kiss on the cheek. Turning to smirk at the chick I caught her rolling her eyes as she took frustrated leave.

"Oh-oh, Mandy, I ah …Hi how was your day? Can I get you a drink?" He stammered.

"A glass of sweet white wine, thanks." We got talking for a while then his phone rang. Here we go excuses,

excuses! I found us a table and waited for him to return. Within minutes of his return yet another hussy was chasing his tale. This man is attracting females like bees to honey. I bristled. Relief washed over me when he suggested we leave. He had perfect timing because if one more chick decided to encroach on my space, I will without hesitation smack someone upside the head.

During the walk back to his car his phone rang again

"Sorry Mandy I have to get this... Hello?.....Ok, I'm on my way home now. Where are you? ..... Right ok, no problem I will be there shortly."

"Is there anything wrong?" I listened to his one sided conversation. Expecting him to do that usual "Man SOS" call I prepared myself to call a cab. When he explained the situation instantly, I thought this guy doesn't have his own place, I bet he's borrowing his friend's flat for the night.

The drive back to his place was short. The conversation was limited as we both enjoyed the vibe, we made jokes and reminisced on our younger years; the days of people sized sweat prints being left on the wallpaper at a *shoobs*. For those of you that don't know what a shoobs is, it's an all-night party, normally in someone's house.

The DJ on the radio was playing slow jams. "This DJ is playing some jams tonight!" I exclaimed dancing in the seat. My vagina was reacting to the music. I felt her moistening.

"Come on, let's continue this inside." His place was a neat little studio flat. Can I get you another drink?" He walked into the kitchen and came back with a couple glasses, placing them on an end table before turning on the music. He pulled me into his arms we started slow dancing.

He had two left feet and his grind was off but the music and alcohol had me feeling some kind of way. We laughed and joked before he started kissing on my neck. His shaft rubbed on my stomach.

"It feels like someone's getting excited to see me!" I slurred. He bashfully apologised. His embarrassment turned me right on. I grabbed his belt and dropped his pants. I looked at his banana head. Oh dear, he's not circumcised. I thought. I pulled his skin back and started working that boy. Placing a condom in my mouth I pulled that sheaf right down over his manhood.

A sound of relief above my head encouraged me into deep throat action. His legs started to shake the more I worked him.

"Oooo shit woman! Come here." He pulled me to my feet hoisted my dress above my ass and lifted me. I wrapped my legs firmly around his neck while he ate my vagina.

For a skinny guy he was strong. Before long I was moaning into the ceiling. This boy was no amateur with his tongue. "I need some dick!" I shrieked when I felt the approach of my long awaited climax. Releasing me from his shoulders he spun me around, bending at my waist I spread my legs giving him maximum entry.

I shook my ass as he pounded my pussy, his cock grazing my spots. I backed my ass up on him over and over again. His intense slapping of my cheeks increased the ferocity of our actions. My ass jiggled violently with his deep thrusts. I searched for something to steady myself, my head repeatedly banged against the wall.

His moan rented the room as he shouted. "I'm cummingggg!"

Pushing him backwards into the chair I rode him, my vagina cried and begged for release.

"Ohhh shit woman you feel ....ooooo ....ggrrrrrr." I

peeked over my shoulder. His nails dug into my hips. His eyes rolled back. "Aagrhghhhhshyhjsyhajnsjdkmd." I felt his load explode. It was over.

I felt his body relax and his cock slide out of me, I climbed off him once I heard his gentle snores. "Another one bites the dust." I muttered quietly retrieving my possessions before letting myself out.

I sat in the cab lost in thought. 'Will I see him again? Probably not! '

The next day I got an email.

Thanks for last night, let's do it again sometime.

Sighing I deleted it.

"How was ya night Dee?"

"It was alright, but homeboy really isn't for me."

"Why what happened?" Her raised eyebrow enquired.

"Conversation got boring. I think I'll give it a week and think of some excuse. Coz he really isn't for me." I replied before walking out the room.

Story 7: Diane & Rick

Rick

Moving can be a bad experience for everyone, but for me it's a new chapter opening. Plus I get to go shopping. 2004 was the perfect year. At twenty-five years young, I was sitting on half a million in the bank, I was in the best physical shape of my life and my cars were on another level.

Rolling up to the furniture store, I observed all the staff beaming at me through the window. Who could blame them it's not every day someone pulls up in an all-black Ferrari F430 with all black 20 inch rims. I was a man that loved to attract people's attention.. Some call me vain, arrogant or even conceited, however when you look as good as me, do you blame me? Standing at 6ft 4in tall, I worked hard to ensure my physique had women turning their heads daily, my kissable lips and dimple, made their lips dribble. Believe me I was not easily missed.

Immediately after I entered the shop a round pudgy, balding, sweaty man approached me

"Good morning Sir, if you need any help please feel free to ask." I could smell his sour breath from three feet away.

"No thanks, Pops! I'm good." I distractedly replied my eyes scoping the showroom. Standing on the far side of the showroom was the reason I came to this joint. My homeboy had mentioned he found some nice furniture in this store; and suggested I take a trip. He also happened to mention a particular sales assistant working there who blew him off and made him feel small. There's no way any girl is going to see me and blow me off like she did my home boy. I love a challenge. My mate was not joking this girl was hot, shoulder length hair, legs I would climb and see where they led me, a sexy ass and I would say double-d breasts.

"Hi, there!" I said gaining her attention; I approached her from behind.

"Good afternoon, sir!" She replied briefly catching my eye before returning her focus on surveying the store. This girl was looking stunning from across the room, she was even more gorgeous up close. I must admit my boy was a little out of his league with this one. Her persona and air of confidence shouted 'Woman in Charge.'

"Sir, sir!" Tantalised by the angel in front of me, I had to get my lines in order.

"Sorry Miss? I didn't catch your name. I was just trying to work out what bed would go better in my place." I enquired.

"Well let me know when you've made up your mind and I will get someone to assist you," She stated politely feigning interest.

"I was thinking you could assist me with this Miss?" I smiled charmingly, with a further attempt to get her name.

"You may call me Diane." Her reply was polite and extremely professional.

"Nice to meet you Diane, I'm Rick!" I winked at her deepening my smile to enhance my dimple.

"I would love to assist you however; I'm rather busy right now. I'm the Manager of the store and I have a lot of work to do! I can get a member of my staff to assist you!" She undoubtedly rejected my flirting.

Turning on her heel she walked away putting distance between us. Being the true predator that I am, her rejection didn't faze me. It merely invoked more interest. Taking a look at myself in one of the many mirrors in the store, I smiled and continued looking around.

Diane's lack of interest and the way she looked at me like she was dealing with any other customer made me shake my head.

"I'm going to get you!" I said to myself. My looks and charm seemed to have no effect on this girl. I tried once more to get her attention, and once again she turned me down. I was starting to have doubts about my game. Discreetly I blew air into my hand to do an odour check, and sniffed under my armpits. Both were fresh. "Maybe she swings the other way." I muttered to myself and continued my search for a bed.

Eventually I found a bed that would fit perfectly. I could not wait to leave this store my self-esteem felt a little crushed.

The drive back to my house took forever, I was getting the attention that I normally received, whenever I drove my Ferrari but I wasn't in the mood to take it in. Shocked by the rejection from a home furniture sales lady really wasn't sitting well with me.

"I don't care how sexy the damn woman is, how dare she reject me. Obviously she just doesn't know who I am!" I said to the empty car. Turning up the music to the sounds of Rick Ross *I'm the Boss* I let the music pound through the speaker system.

Three days later...

Frustration and boredom motivated a brutal *Insanity* workout I was still baffled about the rejection from Diane. I needed to figure out a master plan to get her attention. The music was blasting through the speaker system when it suddenly paused itself as my phone rang, this Bang & Olufsen system was high tech and I loved that feature of muting the music whenever the phone rang.

"Hello!" I answered gruffly and slightly out of breath.

"Good afternoon, may I speak with Mr Fenton please?" A soft yet firm female voice asked.

"Speaking?!" My tone was abrupt and slightly aggressive I was not in the mood to speak to anyone, especially when that someone disturbed my workout.

"Sorry to disturb you Sir, I'm calling from Furniture World about your purchase." Her voice sounded familiar, Diane, my heart began to pound.

"Glad you called Diane, how may I help you." I softened my tone with a smile.

"Mr Fenton, you remembered my name?" Her tone perked up a little.

"Yes, I did how could I not remember such a beautiful name and person?" I turned the charm on.

"Thank you sir, that's so kind." Her tone remained professional.

This girl was too professional for my liking. "I was hoping you would call." I stated with a smile.

"Why is that, Sir?"

"I was hoping to take you out for a drink sometime."

"Mr Fenton let's get something straight. I never mix business with pleasure. Will you be available tomorrow?

Your bed is ready for delivery." Her attitude really rubbed me the wrong way.

"I will be available. Will you deliver yourself with the bed, Ms Diane?" I laughed.

"Your bed will arrive between 8am and midday. Have a good day Mr Fenton." She replied before cutting the call.

"Who the hell does this girl think she is? Blowing me off again! I never get blown off by any chick once let alone twice. The game is on now! I'm going to make sure I get this girl, and show her who is boss no matter what!" I grunted and resumed my squat thrusts.

To my surprise ten minutes after putting the phone down and getting back to my workout my phone rang again.

"Hello?!" The tone of my voice was harsh, who is this? I thought to myself not recognising the number.

"Hi Rick, its Diane."

"Diane?" Surprise, surprise, I thought to myself.

"Yes Diane, about that drink pick me up at eight!" Before I could get a word in she ended the call. This girl is hard work. I thought to myself but I love a challenge. My mood instantly changed I was back in the game again.

I parked outside Diane's work place a few minutes before eight and took the time to scan my music selection. Deciding on the soothing tones of D'angelo, I waited for Diane to finish work.

Diane

From my vantage point I observed the store. I had been Regional Manager for a while, and this particular branch wasn't meeting its targets. Too many staff members sitting on their asses, and not enough hustling was the problem. I had just completed a store wide overhaul from staff to old stock.

"MIKE! MIKE! Take your eyes out my cleavage, and get involved with straightening the children's department." Bashfully Mike's pale cheeks turned bright red as he scurried to the other side of the showroom. "It's going to be a long day." I said to myself.

I walked downstairs just as a black Ferrari pulled up outside. The driver disembarked, wearing a long diamond chain to his waist, dressed in all black, looking like a rapper. He adjusted his Aviators before shutting the car door and strode towards the entrance. Rolling my eyes I continued organising the rota for the coming week. Out of the corner of my eye I noticed him approach me.

"May I help you?" I asked. He stood there starry eyed staring at me without a reply. "SIR, SIR, MAY I HELP YOU?" I shouted obviously this dude is deaf.

"Sorry Miss ... I'm just trying to work out which bed would be better in my place."

"Well, let me know when you've made a decision I will get someone to assist you." I sat back down and began tapping into my computer. He stood there talking, obviously trying to make small talk. Don't people get it? I have work to do, I have no time for chit chat.

Obviously he wasn't going to get the message, I walked away and called John over to assist him with his purchase. I could feel his eyes following me. "Maybe I should put my ring back on." Every single male that comes into this place tries to hit on me. I'm so not ready. It had been two years since Rasheed had passed away and I had thrown myself into working. Within two years I had gone from store assistant to Regional manager, and was the youngest at 24 in the entire company. I observed the team as they scuttled around, attempting to get the commission of the man in the Ferrari. Throughout the day Rick constantly popped into my mind. He was kind of cute.

For the next couple of days I couldn't stop thinking about him. His persistence and his aura sparked something in me. I took the opportunity to call him when his bed arrived. His tone threw me off, as did his loss of breath. I must have caught him at a bad time. He surprised me when he recognised my voice and remembered my name. To hide my fluster when he asked me out, I quickly got off the phone, shutting him down.

Yet thoughts of him crowded my mind for the next 10 minutes so I called him back.

Rick

Diane entered the car, without a comment or look of admiration. Who gets into a Ferrari and doesn't even blink? Diane sat in the passenger seat; she didn't seem impressed at all.

"So where are you taking me for this drink Mr Fenton?" Her tone clipped with professionalism and what sounded like a lack of interest.

"Please call me Rick!"

"Sorry Rick." I glanced over at her, she was looking hot in her pencil skirt and blazer. Did I hear sarcasm? I thought to myself.

"There is a lovely bar in Chingford we could go to, called Sunny's." Sunny's was my bar and if it did not impress Diane nothing else would.

I opened the door for her like a true gentlemen. She stepped inside and stopped as the hostess offered to take her coat. I was greeted like royalty by my staff. The place was managed by my sister, and I had an office upstairs.

"What would you like to drink Diane?"

"A Martini and Coke please." She said looking around, her face was expressionless and I was struggling to read her. I decided to attempt to impress her with my cocktail making skills. I went behind the bar and got creative; I served our drinks with just a little bit of flare.

"Are you friends with the owner?" she asked with a smile when I placed her drink in front of her.

"No Diane! I own the place."

"I see."

She said with a slight nod of her pretty head. Was that a nod of approval? Finally it seems I had her attention for once just letting her know what lane I role in. The fast lane baby! The conversation with Diane was very interesting she seemed to be an intelligent young lady, with a game plan to success; not allowing anyone or anything to get in her way.

"Diane, are you single?" I asked

"Wow." She laughed.

"Did I say something funny?"

This woman really had me feeling unsure of myself.

"Not really, it's just that you ask me out for drinks,

take me to your bar and then you ask if I'm single. It's the reverse order of how things are done, that's cute."

Amusement lit up her pretty face. I couldn't resist giving her a diamond white smile.

"So you find me cute Diane?"

"No Rick! I'm saying the way you do things is cute."

She smirked. Her facial expressions were coming alive. She was no longer a blank doll. I learned a little about this young lady.

"Well I'm not single I've been dating someone for a year now, but nothing serious."

"How can you be dating for year but it's not serious?" I watched her shift in her seat, I could see the wheels churning as she contemplated how much information she intended to give me.

"Well if you must know the guy I'm seeing is a white guy and we've never had sex."

"Are you serious why is that?" I asked.

"We don't need to! Besides he's content just eating me." She stated matter of factly. I was blown away by her admittance of being in an interracial relationship, so many beautiful black women out here are leaving us black men alone, I wonder why?

"I mean what kind of relationship is that?" I questioned.

"Well he is under the impression he has a small dick and if we sleep together I would not enjoy it so we don't."

"I get the feeling there is more to this story." I pushed for more, hoping she wouldn't shut me down.

"What do you mean Rick?" She batted her long lashes innocently. I erupted into laughter, and let it go.

After a few more cocktails I broached the subject again.

"Is there a secret someone you're not talking about?"

She looked at me quizzically before replying, she sighed.

"So you like girls over guys then?"

Fascinated and dejected I looked at her with such intensity she couldn't maintain eye contact. Finding a piece of imaginary lint she mumbled.

"Why would you say such a thing?"

"Well it's just your lack of interest when I asked to take you out. Obviously you can't be into guys if you rejected me." I felt hostile when reality sank in.

"Rick, darling it takes a lot more than a handsome guy like yourself; a pretty car and a bar to impress me. My last boyfriend was a very rich man so material things don't impress me." A hint of a smile crept across her face before she mumbled. "Yes. Her name's Daisy we have been doing our thing for a couple of months now. She's my sister's best friend and my sister would die if she ever found out our secret. Anyway enough about me, how about you player; what's your story?"

"My story is simple. I'm single trying to find Miss Right." I wondered more about this woman, something she said just didn't seem to be sitting right!

"I'm going to the ladies room." She said, collecting her bag off the table.

"You can use the one in my office its much better." I took her hand and led the way.

"Why is that?"

"Well, it's only used by one person." I chuckled.

"I see." I caught her reflection in the mirror and smiled.

"Let's go, I'll show you."

"Thanks." I led the way through the door beside the bar and up the wrought iron staircase.

We walked to my office, my thoughts filled with admiration and amazement. How can this pretty girl not have had any dick in two years? I'm going to have to assist this young lady in her time of need.

"The facilities are just behind that door." I stood and gazed down through the full length window. From this view I watched the people on the dance floor. I didn't hear when Diane returned into the room.

"Rick!" She called.

I spun round Diane was wearing a sheer black Basque with stockings, suspenders with some high heels. My mouth dropped to the floor. I had noticed Diane's handbag was a bit big when I picked her up but who was I to judge? It had all become clear.

"Well hello." I whistled she was absolutely stunning. Her sexy walk towards me in the middle of the room matched that of Tyra Banks, in fact she reminded me of Tyra.

"Am I dreaming?" I had to pinch myself to make sure this was real. What a sudden change of events.

Diane sat on my desk with her legs apart and motioned me to come close, loosening my shirt I sauntered towards her. I knew I had game. I should never have doubted myself.

"Get down on your knees and tongue fuck me!"

Shock rippled through me, was this girl for real? I studied her expression; she sat unmoving on the edge of my desk. I thought of my options. The battle within me didn't last very long. How could I refuse this beautiful, arrogant woman?

My tongue began to hurt after half hour of licking, every time I tried to pull away her thighs locked around my head, yet she still hadn't come. Lifting her up in one swift movement, I swept the desk clear and dove deep inside her. I fucked her hard. I drove my cock so deep into her.

Dismay rooted within me, this woman was accepting my pounding and barely moaning. I felt a bit sorry for her, the fact she had no dick for two years and was getting drilled by nine inches of thickness all up inside her.

Diane's constant demands for me to fuck her harder sealed her fate. I unleashed all reservations and all inhibitions. I forced the full length of my raft inside her. It took a while before she began to move, she was wiggling all over my desk her screams increased in volume.

This woman acted like she could handle this dick, her demands to be fucked incensed me. Ask and you shall receive rang through my mind. Her sweet pussy was tight; her juices flowed like a river. I climbed onto the desk and hit it from the back, doggy style. Watching her ass jiggle as she backed it onto me, her screams for more had me shoot my load hard up inside of her. It's a good thing the office is sound proofed otherwise the entire bar would have been banging on my door.

Silence echoed around the room, I watched Diane get dressed. I got the impression that Diane was filled with regret. She didn't say more than a few words after asking me to drop her to her car.

The next day I received a telephone call from Diane asking me to come to the store to collect a gift she had bought me. A gift? I must have laid the pipe down if she was buying me gifts already. I drove down across town to her store. When I got there a member of staff gave me a package. I accepted it and got back in the car. There was a note attached.

"Rick I'm sorry for what happened yesterday it should never have happened I'm not into guys anymore".

I can't believe she tried to give me an aftershave as a

sorry present damn I got played.

Diane

Looking around the luxury sports car brought back memories. I hadn't sat in a Ferrari since Rasheed's death. It was still hard on me. It had been six months since I had last been back to our house. Maybe I should take a trip to our home in Italy, it's long overdue. Sighing to myself, I tried to relax in the company of Mr Fenton; who was obviously trying hard to impress me. He was cute. Not much of a gentleman; imagine I had to open the car door myself. Sigh.

The journey was short to our destination. I had heard about Sunny's from a few of my girlfriends. They had tried to get me to pass through there. I guess now I can see what the hypes all about. The interior was dim, cosy and surprisingly busy for a Wednesday night. I watched in surprise as Rick helped himself to our drinks. Quite impressed when he mentioned he owned the bar, I guess he may not be a drug dealer after all. It's a shame he's working so hard to impress me. Let me let him think what he likes. I didn't feel like sharing much information about who I was.

Growing up in old money meant I wanted for nothing, and needed even less. I lived under the rouse of Diane Palmer, Regional Manager of Furniture World; a humble young lady, who worked all the time. Not Stephanie Windsor-Michaels of Monte Carlo, great grand-daughter and sole heir to a diamond and oil tycoon. I had travelled the world since the day I was born. Life had changed after losing my dear, Rasheed. I would never love again.

Rick Fenton was new money; he seemed quite self-absorbed and obviously hadn't been told no by a female in a long time.

After an hour of talking, I was starting to get bored; I concocted both the story of my white kitty muncher and Daisy, my lesbian lover to spike his interest, to see how he would react. The Martinis were warming my libido and my little lady was beginning to sing. As if reading my mind Rick invited me into his office.

Rick had been caressing my soft spot, on my arm, all evening and the fire was lit within. The alcohol had numbed my guilt for desiring the urge to fuck. My vixen was raving mad; she had not been filled for over two years, by a hard cock and was determined to get some tonight. His expression was priceless, when I stepped out the ladies room in stockings and suspenders with a sheer Basque, matching crotchless and nippleless bra set. Dressing up in sexy lingerie was an everyday thing for me. Since losing Rasheed, it was the only interest I had, outside of being Diane Palmer. I wonder if this guy's tongue works as well eating as it does talking. My mind travelled as he worked, his tongue technique was a B minus. After 30 minutes I began to feel sorry for him.

"Get that cock up in here!" He pushed everything off the desk, and I raised my legs above his head and waited for him to fill me up.

He was moaning and screaming like a bitch by the time I flipped him over and started riding him.

"That's it girl ride my anaconda, fuck me u dirty bitch." He groaned. Looking around I found a stress ball on his desk. I pushed it into his mouth.

"You talk too damn much, just shut up and fuck me." His eyes opened wide with shock as he bent me over the desk and humped me. To say I was happy when he pulled out, with his limp dick in his hand, and collapsed on the chair was an understatement.

I was so annoyed at myself I really should have kept my clothes on.

Granted I had lied at first about being with another woman, I just enjoyed watching his facial expressions, when his mind clogged up with images of me and this Daisy chick. I was hoping it would make the sex better. Guess I was wrong. To top it off his after sex funk, was a turn off. Within minutes of cleaning myself up in his office bathroom, I stood in the door way with my arms across my chest.

"Rick, I have an early start tomorrow, can you drop me to my car please."

"Thank you for a good night out Diane, let's do it again soon." He looked so hopeful like a sated puppy dog after a belly rub.

"Mmm, yes I'll call you, bye!" I hopped out of his car and power walked to mine.

The next day...

"Hi Rick, its Diane, I'm really sorry about last night it shouldn't have happened. I'm a lightweight with alcohol and I lost control. Please pass by my store when you get a chance." I left a voicemail on his phone and went about my day. Surprisingly he turned up 20 minutes later.

"I was in the area when I got your message don't worry about last night. I had a great time." Lowering my eyes, I wondered how I would break it to him.

"Look I can't see you again. I'm... I'm just not into

guys anymore. Thank you for coming. I have to get back to work." I said as I walked back inside my office. I watched while James, one of my sales team, handed Rick the package I had left wrapped up for him.

Total regret ate away at my insides. Every man would be compared to my one true love. Dear God, why did you take him away from me? I buried myself into a pile of papers on my desk and prayed that Rah would forgive me for my indiscretion.

Story 8: Micha & D'Jean

Micha

"The doctor informed me that I would need physiotherapy for a while." I had broken my leg coming off my motorbike.

"Frankly Micha you are lucky to be alive." My mother's worry mixed with her usual sarcasm echoed through the speaker phone.

"Yes ma, I know, I'm lucky to be alive. So physio for a while isn't a bad thing, as long as I can get back on my Ducati; which has been repaired and is waiting in my garage for me to saddle up and ride again." I sighed while rolling my eyes at the phone.

"Don't roll your eyes at me young lady, fix your face. Micha you are not getting back on that death trap!! I cannot bear the thought of losing you. Do you know how scared I was when I got the call from the hospital telling me you were involved in a road traffic accident? Do you?" She literally screamed at me.

"Mum, I'm ok. Please don't worry." Exasperated I looked at the phone while my mother continued to lecture me. We had the same conversation every day for the past six weeks. "Look ma, I've got to go, the door just knocked. I love you."

"Ok Micha, call me later." I could hear the disappointment and hurt in my mother's tone.

I loved her, but sometimes she really does go on. "Ok

2 Sides 2 the Story

will do Ma, take care." I hung up the phone and opened the door.

My mouth dropped to the floor. Oh my... damn...

"Hello, I'm here for Micha."

"I'm Micha, you must be D'Jean." I opened the door wider allowing him access to the hallway.

"That's me, let me get my equipment out the van, I will be right back."

Mesmerised by his stunning hazel eyes, his caramel complexion and his wide shoulders, I couldn't believe this guy was going to be my physiotherapist.

I waited by the door until he came back. "Please follow me." I led him into the living room. "I hope you have enough space to set up." I said stepping aside to allow him into the open plan living room. I waited while he looked around.

"You have a nice home." He commented.

His eyes lingered on the nude painting of me on the back of my Ducati, which hung over the fire place. He smiled.

"Micha, while I set up please complete the form for me, then we can begin."

Sitting down on the couch, I watched him bend over; his ass was round and firm in his adidas tracksuit bottoms. I watched his muscles rippled with every movement.

"Ummm it's a bit warm in here, do you mind if I take off my sweatshirt?"

"Please feel free to make yourself at home. Can I get you a drink?"

"No, I'm fine, thanks." Quickly averting my eyes from his bulging biceps, I continued to fill out the form.

After a series of examinations assessing the damage to

my body, D'Jean guided me to the massage table.

"I will leave the room, please strip down to your panties. Once you've finished please hop on the couch and cover yourself with the towel. Then call me when you are done."

The very first time he touched my body energy sparked and I was hot and wet. His hands were so soft and gentle, but firm as they travelled up and down my body. With every touch, I wished he would slip his fingers between my lips and massage my clit. I had never experienced a massage that literally had me climaxing in ecstasy from the mere touch alone. An hour went by so quickly it was amazing. So much so, I couldn't get up.

That was a month ago, and I had been seeing D'Jean twice a week. For the past two sessions, his fingers had accidently brushed my lips. Today however something was different. He lifted my leg in the air, to rest it on the table to support my body, and worked the tight muscles around my groin. His fingers grazed my clit. I felt his manhood rise as it pressed into my ass. If only he knew how much the pleasure and pain was turning me on.

D'Jean

Holding down two jobs was great financially but my body was screaming for some rest. Getting back home at three in the morning and having to get back up for work at seven was becoming difficult. The money I got from my Physiotherapy job was ok but not for my lifestyle. Let's just say, I enjoy the finer things in life and rather than hit the streets to get my money, I choose to work for my keeps. Being a therapist by day and a stripper at night, the money was very good and I could afford anything my heart desired.

My alarm went off at seven in the morning, causing me to jump. I'm so tired. I yawned really wishing I could stay in bed for another couple of hours. I'm not the type of person to be in an office doing a normal nine to five, hence the reason I chose to be a freelance therapist. I could choose my hours and also choose my clients. My work is usually emailed to me by the private hospital that I represented. My work ethic and technique had acquired me the opportunity to get first choice of clients. The joys of fucking the boss could have its perks.

My latest client email stated I had three new clients, one of which caught my eye. "Micha Harris. Hold up I know this girl." I exclaimed. We went to school together, but I bet she won't remember me. Micha was a rich hotty her parents were loaded and she lived the high life. She had always been that girl that everyone wanted or hated because of the way she looked and conducted herself. She wasn't that girl that got a reputation for sleeping with every boy in school. In fact Micha barely even spoke to the boys; she was always stuck in a book.

I remember trying to speak to her years ago but she totally ignored me. I wasn't the most popular guy in school, I was tall but very skinny and most girls didn't give me a second look, things have changed now. After school I made it a mission to get my body in shape and make girls like Micha beg to be with me.

I knew Micha was rich but not that rich. Her Mansion was on a new complex set on twenty acres of land. The only entrance was via a security guard at the main gates who explained the way to Micah's out house. I drove up to her mansion driveway and a sudden wave of nerves overcame me. I'm guessing she lived with her parents but had her own area of the estate for herself. Her dad must be into cars. There were three Ferraris on the drive. A red California, a grey F430 and a brand new 458 Italia, this man has great taste, I whistled circling the customised Italian cars before heading to the front door.

"Hello, I'm here for Micha."

"I'm Micha, you must be D'Jean."

I was right she doesn't remember me; her lack of recognition was exactly what I wanted. I really didn't want her to remember the lanky haphazard kid from school. I gathered my equipment out the van totally lost in thought. Dazed and stunned it's been a few years since I last laid eyes on Micha, she had developed into an even more stunning lady. She was even hotter than I remembered. Her body was fully shaped. Micha Harris is truly mesmerizing. Her curves were in all the right places. Something about the way she looked at me said she was feeling what she saw too.

"Opportunity equals time and place." I muttered to myself before walking back inside.

I went through the standard preliminary consultation, with the entire form filling process and prepared the massage table. I had to remind myself that as beautiful as she was I needed to remain professional for now. I waited while she settled herself on the table before warming my hands with the oils. This woman is perfect I've done my fair bit of massages in the last three years, but no one had a body like this; not a single mark on her body, a perfect back and bum! Even though she had broken her leg, she had healed flawlessly. She was absolutely stunning.

I found myself looking between her naked flesh and the huge photo of her posing naked on the back of a Ducati. I assumed the photo was airbrushed at first. But now that I was touching her, my eyes were not deceiving me. She truly was perfection.

"Micha, are you sleeping darling?" My alarm had gone off a while ago signalling that the session was over, however I could not pull myself away.

"Sorry, I felt so relaxed." She attempted to get up.

"Don't rush to get up just yet. Once I leave the room take your time. Not to worry most people do fall asleep, it's a good thing it shows your relaxed and comfortable around me." I stopped her from getting up and quickly turned and walked out the room, giving her and myself some space.

That was our first session, several weeks ago. We had been seeing each other twice a week for intense therapy sessions. I could tell Micha was into me, the more we had our sessions, the more she tried to impress me. My game plan was simple, I was going to make this girl want me the way I wanted her back in school. There had been many occasions when I wanked then and even now thinking of her. Now I had her body in my hands. I could only imagine how she felt on the inside.

Today was different, I don't know what or why but the energy in the room had shifted. It seemed like Micha was up to something. There were more candles than normal lit up around the room. She had put on some soft music not our usual sounds of nature CD.

"May I ask the occasion?" Curiosity seeped into my voice.

"What do you mean?" She replied innocently.

"Well the candles and music?"

"I've had a hard week. My pain levels are slightly higher than normal. So I have been trying to relax all day." Her explanation soothed my line of questioning for a few minutes.

"As you wish, you are the client." I commenced our usual routine; Micah's back was knotted as were her legs. She was complaining about the pain in her groin, so I proceeded to release the knotted tissues in her quads. I realised she had exchanged her boy shorts for a thong, 'Could this girl be up to something?' I questioned myself while I worked. Her moans were gentle, her breathing lithe.

"Can you turn over please, so I can work on the other side of your legs?" I worked my way up her legs I could hear her groaning my finger touched her wet lips by mistake, she didn't say anything nor did she open her eyes. I continued to work her legs.

Micha

I couldn't resist all these games were driving me crazy. At night I dreamed of him; during the day all I could do was fantasize over the thought of him. My B.O.B. was dying faster than it had in a long time.

His fingers were hesitant at first when I looked him in his eyes it was all over. I saw the fire within them as his confidence grew with his manhood. He worked my clit bringing me so close to orgasm in a matter of minutes. Every muscle and nerve ending screamed with pleasure as he stroked me over, and over again. He took control of my body like it belonged to him.

I pulled away from his grip long enough to drop the towels on the floor and pull down his tracksuit. Surprised he had no underwear on. His long manhood stood to attention, gripping it with one hand I pulled that cock between my breasts; titty fucking him as he worked my clit.

Straddling the table he climbed on top of me. With his dick in my face I followed suit, when I felt his tongue lick my pulsating pearl. I licked my lips and licked that caramel chocolate lollipop; gagging a few times from his length and pace of his grinding hips. I locked my thighs around his head. His tongue dove into my warm juice box. Beads of perspiration rolled off our bodies as the fire burned. Never before had I received such an intense pussy licking. My climatic scream was muffled by his nine inches of girth and pumping semen. Managing to ease him out my mouth before I choked I sucked on his balls while he continued to ejaculate his load over my breasts.

He clamped my clit between his lips and sucked hard as my juices rocketed out of me. Our bodies quivered as the orgasm subdued.

"WOW!" The only word I was barely able to whisper, on a sigh of contentment. Rolling off the table we collapsed on the mats. His hand lazily dancing on my thigh, as I lazily licked his nipples. His eyes rolled back with a Cheshire cat smile. Thirty minutes later he was packed up and walking out the door.

"Micha you know the drill go and lay down and relax that was an intense workout."

"Same time, next week?" I laughed.

D'Jean

Touching her clit the second time was no mistake. I intentionally teased her clit with my finger she started to moan with pleasure. I then placed my other hand under her bum and finger fucked her backdoor, simultaneously rubbing her clit with my other hand. We positioned ourselves in the sixty-nine position. I could tell she was struggling with my length, however mercy was not an option for this girl. My desire and need to reduce her to a quivering mess was long overdue. We carried on licking and sucking until we both busted our load. Micha was hoping I fucked her, but not today I had to continue my mind games with this girl. Life is a bitch, a man needed to be in control at all times. I'm ready for us to wait it out. Besides I couldn't deny the chemistry between us. She really had me intrigued.

Story 9: Ted & Anabelle

Anabelle

I stood at the bus stop deep in thought. I wasn't in a hurry; I really didn't feel like going straight home. The arguments between my sister and her boyfriend were driving me crazy. The downfall of flat sharing, I sighed. I turned the volume up as *Deborah Cox's* song: *Nobody's supposed to be here* played. I started singing along, totally absorbed in the moment. Startled by the round of applause from the crowd of people who were standing at the bus stop my face turned beet red. It was one of those moments I wished the ground would open up and swallow me whole. I couldn't believe I had got so lost in thought with this melody, to sing in public.

"Nice pipes!" A deep baritone whispered from behind me. Those two words made me cream myself. His voice had a beautiful sexy seductive tone.

"Tha-anks." I stammered turning to see where the voice came from. Standing behind me was a 5'10ish chocolate brother in a bus driver uniform. He was round like a bear, but something about his round face; dimples and his smile made me wanna just curl up in his arms. I had seen him a few times driving the 341 bus.

"You can sing for me any time." He smiled shyly. I blushed, I wanted to come up with a witty comment, the spellbinding way this guy looked at me left me speechless.

"I'm just about to get off my break let me take you to your stop." He motioned for me to follow him.

"Hmmm, okay." I followed him to his bus and climbed on.

"What's your name?" I whispered.

"Ted, what's yours?"

"Anabelle."

"Nice to meet you beautiful Anabelle." He reached for my hand and kissed the back of it, causing a rosy red to glaze my cheeks again.

I sat in comfortable silence for a few minutes while he did his checks and I listened to *Aaliyah's One in a million.*

"Baby you don't know what you do to me...." I started singing again I just couldn't stop myself. He was outside the bus talking to his colleague.

"I feel a chemistry... Anabelle can I get your number? Then take you to dinner?" His baritone came out smooth with bass.

"Oh my..."

"You can call me 07949 117488." I sang.

We sang verses the entire journey, fortunately the bus was empty and only a few people hopped on and off for the fifteen minute ride.

I hopped off the bus at my stop blew him a kiss, and danced down my road. I ran into the house.

"Crystal, where are you?" I shouted.

"In the kitchen, where's the fire?" She asked, rushing out the kitchen her hands covered in flour.

"OH! MY! GOD! I met this guy today, he's amazing!! We sang together on the bus. OMG I can't wait to see him again." I swooned the words tumbled out my mouth without taking a breath. I was so excited. I ran upstairs to my bedroom, on the way to my room, my phone rang.

"Helloooo." I sang.

"Anabelle it's me, your Teddy Bear." He sang.

"Oh hi, Teddy Bear, how you doing?" I asked pushing the door closed behind me.

I flopped across the bed, enjoying the way his voice seduced me. The more he talked the wetter I became. I found my fingers beginning to massage my lower lips. My fingers strummed a rhythm to his melodic voice. With my eyes closed I played with my pebble hard nipples. Imagining his tongue trailing along my neck, between the verses of songs he was singing to me.

"Oh baby." I moaned. In a trance I reached in my bedside draw and pulled out my bullet. My breathing intensified.

Ted

Growing up in the church we all had to sing. I never enjoyed singing growing up, however as I got older I realised the benefits of a good voice. Plus the girls loved it when I sang to them.

Another twelve hour shift, this job is really getting to me. The only reason I hadn't quit were the perks it came with. The salary was comfortable, and the opportunity to obtain three to four new numbers a week from all these pretty women. The best thing I don't need to go out to the clubs to get them; Young or old they all came to me.

Pulling my bus up to the bus termination point, to take my break, I saw this beauty standing at the bus stop. The bus only ran every half an hour on this route so I knew I would have enough time to get to know her. Her back was turned to me so she didn't see me approach her. I stood behind her enjoying the view. She started to sing; what a beautiful voice. Her head phones where in her ears and she was singing quite loud. I don't think she realised, she truly was engrossed in the music. When she had finished singing the song a round of applause made her jump. She spun around everyone at the bus stop was clapping and cheering. I found the way she turned red so attractive.

"Nice pipes." I stated so only she could hear.

"Tha-anks." She blushed even more.

"I've seen you around before, you are beautiful." I couldn't help compliment her. I had been scoping her for a while, and I just hadn't had the courage to approach her.

"Yes, you may have." She lowered her lids and smiled.

"I'm just going on a break but I could give you a lift to your stop if you want?" I hoped she said yes, I really wanted the opportunity to get to know her.

"That would be nice."

She made herself comfortable on the luggage rack opposite my driver's seat. This girl could not stop singing but her voice was lovely and I wasn't about to stop her. Vocally our voices harmonised so naturally. We sang song after song until we arrived at her destination. I couldn't let her leave without getting her number. I watched as she hopped off my bus running to a house.

The rest of my day was just perfect I had a smile on my face all day and I could not wait to give Anabelle a call.

"Helloooo." Her angelic voice sang.

"Anabelle it's me, your Teddy Bear" I sang.

"Oh hi, Teddy Bear how you doing?" We spoke in our sing songy way for a while. I really was enjoying her conversation. I could get used to this.

"I'm just relaxing in bed thinking of you, and was hoping you would call. Most guys normally take a few days to ring and I hate that. If I give a guy my number, I want him to use it.." She grumbled.

"I'm not most guys, darling!" I replied sarcastically.

"I can tell!" I could hear her smile through the phone.

We spoke for hours and the conversation just felt natural. We spoke about everything and nothing. It didn't feel like we had just met. I felt like I had known her all my life. This girl is so real! I thought to myself. Anabelle had me dripping just by the tone of her voice.

"Anabelle?" her toned had become mere wisps of air.

"Yes babe?"

"Are you ok you've gone quiet all of a sudden?" I enquired.

"Yes Teddy Bear, your voice is so deep and smooth; I didn't wanna interrupt your talking. Your voice is sexy and you are really turning me on right now." She stated.

"What are you doing babes?" My imagination began to run laps.

"Do you really wanna knnooowww?"

"Yes, please." I held my breath and waited.

"I'm playing with myself!" She crooned.

"Are you really?" I exhaled; this girl is fucking amazing.

"Yes. What phone do you have?" I asked eagerly.

"Why?"

"I would love to FaceTime you so we both can pleasure each other, you know cybersex." I replied.

"Oh I've never done that before, I have an iPhone." She sounded anxious and intrigued at the same time.

"Ok, I will FaceTime you." I cut the call and dialled her back.

Anabelle

The call was connected, at first the picture was dark, nerves floated in my stomach like butterflies. I had never had cybersex; I honestly don't know what had come over me. It had been 4 years, since I had a boyfriend. I waited for him to turn on the light in his room.

"Can you hear me? Are you there?" I asked nervously.

"Yes babes. Can I see what I'm missing?" Biting the bullet, I lowered the phone to rest between my thighs. I was lying flat on my back with my legs shaped like a diamond.

"Dammmm girl you have a big clit and your pussy is so wet." He commented his voice had dropped a few decibels making it even huskier.

"It's your fault entirely." I sang. I flicked my clit, inserting my fingers just a little and withdrew them, a string of pussy juice trailed behind.

"Really? Taste yourself for me. Damn you're making me hard."

"Can I use my toy?" I laced my voice with innocence, I practically begged for permission.

"Feel free; don't let me stop your fun." I watched him whip out his short thick cock and begin to stroke.

"Aww, aww, awww Ted." I was so turned on. My clit pulsed with electricity.

"Yes?"

"Does that feel good? Do you like what you see?" I moaned.

"What you're doing is turning me on so badly." His grunts came in rapid session. He stroked to the sound of my bullet racing on my clit.   "I'm coming babes; don't stop ahhhooo, aww awww."

Ted

Anabelle burst out laughing.

"Why are you laughing?" I felt slightly embarrassed as I shot my load over the screen of my phone.

"No..nothing….." She stammered between breaths.

"I just can't believe you got me so worked up!" I replied wiping my phone with my t-shirt.

"Wow, you are a bad boy." She giggled.

"That was quick!"

I wanted the ground to swallow me up she laughed hysterically. I couldn't believe I had released my nut so quickly. It had only been three minutes according to the call duration.

"Look Angel, I got to get cleaned up. Call me later." I hurried to cut the call. I felt so ashamed of myself.

"Ok Teddy, maybe we can meet up sometime." She sounded hopeful.

"Hmmm yea ok, that sounds good. Bye." I cut the call and groaned. Kicking myself for releasing so quickly! This girl really had me so flustered, and ready to plunder. Maybe just maybe I will meet up with her.

Story 10: Melissa & Randy & Shonda

Melissa

Randy sat hunched over his desk crunching numbers, the tension evident in his shoulders, as he organised the payroll for the builders; it was a long and time consuming process. I stood in the door way watching him. He was gorgeous, a slender version of usher. In a yellow sundress I walked around his desk and massaged his shoulders. Something about watching him work turned me on.

Purposefully, I kissed his lips, before he turned back to the books he was working on. I seductively caressed the back of his neck.

"Babe, I got somewhere you can put that." I whispered then licked down his throat.

"Hmmmm do tell." He responded distractedly.

"First, that spot on my neck. You remember that one? Then on my breast one nipple at a time."

The smile on his face melted away the tension in his shoulders. I placed my nipples in his mouth through the cotton dress.

"After which, I will reacquaint myself with my long lost everything then show him how much I've missed him." I smiled, watching him cover his eyes. I loosened the buttons on my dress allowing room for his long pianist's fingers to release my nipples from their braless constraints.

"Ha-ha-ha I will be good I promise!" I watched his eyes light up.

"Hmmm do whatever, feel free your allowed that." He mumbled with his mouth full of my 32DD breasts. Pushing his chair backwards to allow a little more room, I slid down on my knees and unzipped his pants, releasing his manhood from the confines of his slacks; and take him between my lips.

"You know that grinds my gears, no work tonight!" He groaned. I chuckled.

"No baby, do your work. The boys need to be paid. Let me please you while you work your numbers. Watching you hard at work turns me on....sitting here looking sexy deep in thought. We can have our fun tonight." I begin to massage him, preparing him for what's to come later. I rub his cock between my breasts while sucking the tip; licking down his shaft, sucking on the balls and back again. I feel his concentration begin to ebb, especially once the sloshing and purring gets louder. I play with my freshly waxed smooth pussy, she was purring and wet just the way he loved her.

I look up to see his eyes roll back. I feel the first pulses on my tongue, his sweet salty juices beginning to leak as I titty fuck him; stroke him until his load shoots down the back of my throat.

Randy

"Melissa I can't keep doing this!" Agitation and frustration was causing my head to explode. I had a constant headache.

"Yes you can!"

"WHY DO I NEED TO KEEP SLEEPING WITH YOU? I'M A MARRIED MAN! I'M THROUGH WITH

YOU MELISSA." I shouted through gritted teeth.

"Well, it's simple Randy, you do for me and I do for you. How many government contracts have you had in the last five years? All thanks to me! So the choice is yours! You stop doing for me and I stop doing for you, it really is simple."

Her sly tone as she raked her nails down my back infuriated me. All I wanted to do was knock her block off. *How am I going to get this She-devil out of my life?* I groaned running my hands down my face stepping out of her reach.

My business was going downhill before I met Melissa and she is right I need these contracts. Melissa was in charge of all government projects. We met a few years back, at a charity benefit and she hasn't left me alone since. Melissa is a very attractive lady; the perfect catch for any man, if you can handle a cold hearted ruthless bitch; with only herself and her needs on her mind. I was and still am in love with my wife. All this creeping around is taking a toll on me and my health. My stress levels are sending my blood pressure through the roof. But we had bills to pay and a man has to do, what he has to do to get them paid.

My wife was in a car crash a few years back, the impact had shifted several discs in her spine, she had been wheelchair bound for a long time. The total loss of power in her legs had meant she had gone from an independent woman working in Law, in the city to a very dependent woman. It had taken the last year and thousands of pounds worth of treatments to finally get her out of the chair, although she still finds it hard to stand for very long periods of time.

The financial strain to maintain the mortgage, the medical treatments and all the household bills was on my shoulders. No I'm not complaining. It's a man's duty to provide but business wasn't going well especially in the first two years after Shonda's accident. The strain and lack of support had caused me to lose focus. Before her injury we had a very good life style; she was on a very good wage, and business for me was picking up. I had a couple major building contracts and had just purchased a few buildings for renovations. Money was coming in and allowed us to enjoy it; we had expensive taste.

We lived life to the fullest, although we had savings after 2 years money just wasn't the same. Shonda still isn't ready to return to work and I'm struggling to make ends meet hence the reason for Melissa. Melissa became that shoulder I leaned on, she was supportive and offered me a solution. She started sending contracts throughout the city my way, as soon as money started to flow, so did her demands.

At first it was an escort to a function here, or a luncheon there, then sex became her everyday demand. Unfortunately for me she had hidden cameras around her office that caught us on tape, which she was now using to blackmail me. She had threatened to show my wife, and I couldn't handle that, it would destroy her, it would destroy us.

"Melissa, I can't do this anymore. I'm tired and I'd rather go broke than continue this. It's over now, please leave my office." I stood by the door holding it open for her. I watched her collect her purse, adjust her dress and walk out the office; the look on her face was pure evil. It sent a shiver up my spine.

My wife wants us to sell the house and down size but my pride is too big, what will people say? Sitting at my desk going over my payroll for the week my wife walks in, on her crutches, slow steady and absolutely stunning.

My wife is the definition of perfection, I keep telling her that. She would go out of her way to make me happy, and I felt guilty having to cheat on her.

"Hey gorgeous" I stand to meet her sweeping her up into my arms.

"Hey you." She giggled.

"What are you doing here?" I ask. My joy at seeing her overruled by Melissa's departure just minutes before.

"Can I release some of that tension; you're carrying around with you?" She asked, snuggling my neck.

"Err Shonnie, I got a pile of work to do but if you give me 30 minutes I will be all yours?" I said placing her down in her favourite corner by the window in her chaise lounge. That only meant one thing; she was horny. Our love life was perfect, she was a freak and I was up for anything.

"I will be right back. Can I get you a drink or anything?" I asked looking at my wife; she looked fantastic sitting in a fitted white knee length dress, and sandals. Her natural long hair was braided up into what looked like a crown. It was regal, just like her. She looked up from her book and smiled.

"No thank you, my husband. I don't need anything but you."

"Ok my Queen, I will be right back." I couldn't leave the room quick enough.

I hustled to the men's room and stood in front of the sink, scooping up some water I washed my face and looked in the mirror. I was disgusted with myself. I hated the person I had become. Removing my shirt I quickly checked for any incriminating evidence that the She-Devil may have left. I quickly pulled down my slacks and scrubbed my balls. Removing any trace of the She-Devil. I fixed myself up and walked back to my office taking a cleansing breath.

Stopping at the entry way, I watched my woman; she had dozed off in her space. She had turned on some reggae music, and the sounds of Etana filled the air. I couldn't help but smile. I resumed my position at my desk and quickly completed the payroll, and arranged the BACS transfers for all the contractors. Just as I was about to shut down the pc, an email popped up on the screen.

Randy poo, your wife sure is beautiful in her white dress. I see she is starting to swell. She is such a sweet lady.

I quickly deleted the email, emptied the trash and switched off the computer. I picked up her sticks and flung them over my shoulder, scoped up my wife up into my arms I walked out the office, locking the door behind me with a lot of effort trying not to wake her, I took the lift down to the underground car park.

Melissa

People think I'm such a bitch; to be honest I don't give a damn. I have spent years being someone else's doormat, abuse post. I'm tired of people wanting to take me for what I have and not give anything back in return. When Randy said it was over, I felt like my world had shattered. We had been spending time together for the past 4 years. Every other week we went on dinners, luncheons, functions, trips around the country. He had become such a part of my world and I love him. How could he not want to continue and build? He said we would be together; he said he would leave his wife. He said we could start a family. The way he touched me when we made love; the way he kissed me good morning, and good night. The way he held my hips whenever we made love.

"Oh Randy I love you so much, I will do anything to be with you." I said before walking out the door. I don't understand how he can say he was going to give up us and the empire we have built, for that cripple.

I stood in the stairwell watching as she shuffled along, how can I get rid of her? Maybe if I push her down the stairs. Something inside of me snapped. I watched as he ran into the men's room, before I slipped into his office. She was sitting there in the lounge that he never let me touch, like's she's a fucking queen. It was obvious she hadn't heard me; she was bobbing her head to the music. I crept up behind her; she had a glass of water sitting on the table next to her. I had remembered Randy had mentioned she was allergic to nuts. I had emptied a few into my hands and rubbed them over my hands before creeping up behind her and covered her mouth, forcing a nut into her mouth.

She struggled, clawing at my hands, unfortunately for her, her weak ass wasn't a match for me and her sorry attempt at a fight was like that of a two year old. Within minutes her breathing had slowed. I took that as my cue to get out of dodge. I crept back out to the stair well and walked down to the next floor before calling the elevator. I looked in the mirror.

"Girl, you really are working this yellow!" I blew myself a kiss oblivious to the crazy, irrational look in my eyes.

Shonda

I had seen her before, I had heard about her now I

finally had a name to go with the face. Melissa DE Vail. Her name was ringing all over the circuit and my friends kept me in the loop of the comings and goings of the elite circle in the business. It really isn't a big world at all. Randy had often told me she had the key to the contracts, and he was trying to get his scraps. He assumed I was oblivious to the financial struggles we were going through. I also knew about his indiscretions with the tramp. I just wished he would talk to me.

I had stepped off the elevator and overheard the argument between Randy and the high pitched female voice so I had waited in the hall until I heard him open the door, before hiding behind the huge vase filled with flowers. I watched as she attempted to kiss him and he pushed her away. 'Oh Randy!' I couldn't blame him, I could only be angry with myself and the yellow tramp. If it weren't for the accident everything would be ok. I waited a few minutes before making my way to my husband's office. My heart broke when I saw the pain he quickly tried to cover.

The way his eyes lit up when he looked at me had never changed. However the heavy cloud bares the weight of the universe on his shoulders.

I knew the pressure was taking its toll on his health as much as he had tried to hide everything from me. I knew the extent, and as gruelling as the path behind me has been, it is my husband that has motivated me to walk, to move to get out of the wheelchair and return to my former glory. It is my husband that has been the epitome of strength throughout the last 5 years.

"Dear God, please guide us through this. Please help me to help my husband. Let me bare some of the pressure he feels, so we can carry this load together as man and wife. I thank you for my blessings. Amen." I watched my husband walk out the door and I rested my head, I will talk to him when he comes out. I said to myself. I saw her reflection but it was too late, I couldn't breathe.

As she walked past me I recognised her face. As she moved her hand I managed to whisper. "It was you!" As my world became black, a fast memory of the person who had crashed into my car, sending my car careening into a telephone pole.

Randy

My world was no longer worth living. I sat staring into space, after everyone had left. The day had gone by in a blur, from the tears and condolences to the minute they lowered my Queen into the ground. My world had lost its light. A card on the table caught my eye.

"Now we can be together, Love always, M."

To be continued.....

Out word from the Authors

So there you have it.... Thank you for reading this book. Hopefully you enjoyed reading it as much as we enjoyed writing it.

Remember there are always *2 Sides 2 the Story* and more often than not we don't actually think about the other party's feelings. So take your time when it comes to handling people especially after sex. Always practice safe sex!

Tell us your opinion visit our webpage:

www.3icreations.org

Let us know which characters you would like featured in a full length novel. Which characters can you relate to? We value your opinion both good and bad so remember to drop us a line.

Look out for our next book entitled *Creepers* coming soon.

Turn over the page for an excerpt.

Creepers

Membership was by member recommendation and a stringent verification process.

Members were not allowed to speak about what takes place or else they would be removed from the site.

Only the finest of the finest were allowed to play.

The membership fees for women were £2,000 per year.

All men who joined were expected to be uninhibited; open minded and ready to do whatever a woman demanded.

The women on *Creepers* were of a different class, a different breed, compared to the type you get on most dating sites. These women were CEOs of companies or Managing Directors, millionaire house wives, people of likeminded money and they were all women with one thing in common, to which you will find out later. Would you like to know more? May I go on further!

The men were a different story. The guys were willing and able to earn their dues by pleasing these women. Some didn't have a job but it didn't matter, to these ladies that's exactly the type of men they were looking for; men with lots of time on their hands. Men who would give them attention, show them affection, and were willing to be there for them at times when they needed them. If these ladies were married, their husbands tended to be too busy to show them any time or affection and more often than not were too busy having their extra marital affairs to even notice their wives. No matter their marital status these women all had one thing in common. They were lonely.

Every evening ***Creepers*** would open their site and match the profiles to couples or even groups who had or wanted similar things. The men were prohibited to see the women's profiles; however the women can see theirs. The men are given fifteen minutes to woo and convince the women to continue with the conversation. Only once the prospective candidates have caught the women's attention will the women click on the 'Reveal' button granting the man of interest access to view her profile.

As one of the founding members of ***Creepers,*** I didn't find the need to participate in the games, but on occasions I would play along and see what desperate woman I could win over. I was a self-made man, money and women were the least of my worries however boredom was another factor. I often found myself feeling and craving something outside of the box; especially after a hard day's work. By day I ran a successful Architecture Company. Most people smoke or drink in the evenings, the last thing I want is to haul myself out of a bar piss face drunk. I'm pretty much a health freak; my vices are either working out in the gym or working on my dating site.

I must confess I obviously had an upper hand on the other guys. I was privy to what the ladies looked like, I knew enough about their backgrounds that I was able to entertain and gain more profile acceptances than the other male members, so I always chose accordingly and I used what I knew to my advantage.

One thing I've learnt money can buy you many things, but your personality is given not bought. Many of these members really needed a lesson in interpersonal relationship building. They lacked so many things that realistically in the real world I'm surprised they actually achieved success. Anyhow let me not drone on about my pet peeve. Let me get on with telling you more about **Creepers**.

I was told by one of my mates about this lovely lady who was interested in joining the games and I could not wait for her to sign up. She was the owner of a chocolate company. She had been single for a few years, she had no kids and according to him she had a body to die for. Her name was Elaine Jackson.

I knew Elaine, she was a friend of my twin sisters; she was a couple of years older than me. Back then I didn't exist in her eyes. She used to come around to our place when we were younger. I haven't seen or heard about her in years. I remember growing up with the biggest crush on her. I remember once I stole her picture from my sister's photo album, and she became my fantasy girlfriend for years even though we never spoke more than a few words.

Once Elaine had left college I hadn't heard anything about her, I assume my sisters and she had fallen out; what over I had no idea, I never asked and they never told. To say I was pleasantly surprised when my mate had given her a referral, even more so when I saw her request come up on the profile list of the website.

I sat staring at the picture Elaine had put up she had named herself, Mistress of Wax. The name alone made me wonder what had become of my childhood crush. Her looks hadn't changed much. Her hair had been cut into one of those short pixie styles with blonde streaks, her hazel eyes rimmed with a smoky shadow that gave her a seductive mysterious gaze; she reminded me of Stacey Dash. Her lips curved up in a smile exposing her dimples. I continued to flick through her pictures and came across one of her lying on a four poster bed with red silk sheets. Her hair was pulled up into a tight long ponytail, she was bound to the bed with leather ropes, legs spread wide. Standing to the side of the bed someone was holding a candle dripping hot wax over her. Mesmerised I found myself daydreaming of what took place while the photos were being taken.

In my fantasy I became the photographer...

The darkened room mixed with the sweet scent of perfumed candles and body oils engulfed me. I watched as Ms Wax sauntered into the room. Her hair pulled tight in a long ponytail wearing leather thongs and studded nippleless bra with a pair of thigh high studded 6 inch heeled boots, her bright red lips silent. Her confidence exuding her, she was followed by a petite figure dressed from head to toe in a latex body suit and mask; a thick waist shackle attached to the lead in Ms Wax's gloved hand.

No words were spoken between them. Climbing onto the bed my eyes followed through the lens of the camera the rotation of her thick hips and apple shaped ass cheeks were hypnotizing. I couldn't control the throb in my loins. I watched entranced by the slow sensual game Ms Wax and her slave played. The slave licked up Ms Wax's limbs until she was securely tied to the posts of the bed.

The slave pinched and tweaked Ms Wax's nipples before reaching for something on the bedside cabinet. 'I wonder what that is.' I thought curiosity encouraged me to zoom in; the shutters on my camera snapping continuously. The object I realised was clamps. There were three of them. The slave gracefully straddled Ms Wax, not quite touching her body, yet the motion caused her to purr. It wasn't an ordinary purr; she sounded more like a cat having its tummy tickled. I felt my breath hitch in my chest when I witnessed the slave harshly simultaneously clamp both her nipples. Her pain made my pleasure increase. I had never witnessed a photo shoot opportunity like this. I watched holding my breath. My camera was constantly snapping, not wanting to miss a single shot.

Find out what happens next when **Creepers** is released.

Authors Bios

C.C. Downer

C.C was born and lives in London, England. She is a mother of two and a busy entrepreneur. Family is her number one priority.

C.C.'s dream has always been to write books, although fear prevented her from doing so. Her decision to finally publish her work came after years of family and friends encouraging her to give the world an opportunity to experience her creativity. So when Alvonne approached her to work with him to create *2 Sides 2 the Story* she knew it was the perfect time to make her dream come alive.

2 Sides 2 the Story is her first published manuscript. Her next book *Chocolate Thrills & High Heels* will be released in the summer of 2014.

Alvonne Locker

Alvonne Locker was born and raised on the beautiful island of Montserrat, in the West Indies. A volcanic eruption on the island forced Alvonne and his family to evacuate the island and move to Walthamstow, East London. This dramatic experience changed the course of his life forever, forcing him to embrace a new world, which was far removed from his humble beginnings. Choosing not to be a product of his environment and he seized the opportunities available to him.

Alvonne has become an established and hardworking business man.

The next step was to pursue his lifelong dream of writing his first novel. Alvonne identified a gap in the market and *2 Sides 2 the Story* was born. The book explores the male and female perspective of intimate experiences through a series of short stories.